CEES NOOTEBOOM was born in The Hague in 1933. He is a poet and the author of several novels and travel books, many of which are illustrated by his wife, the photographer Simone Sassen. His first international success came when *Rituals* was awarded the Pegasus Prize in 1983, which led to its publication in the United States. Later, following the success of *Berlijnse Notities* (published in English as *Roads to Berlin* in 2012), Cees Nooteboom was awarded the German Order of Merit. In 1993 he won the Aristeion European Literature Prize for *The Following Story*, which confirmed his reputation as a prominent figure in contemporary European and world literature. His novels including *Rituals*, *All Souls* and *The Foxes Come at Night*, and the travel narrative *Roads to Santiago*, have subsequently been translated into many languages. He now lives in Amsterdam and on the island of Minorca.

INA RILKE is the prize-winning translator of books by Erwin Mortier, Tessa de Loo, Dai Sijie and Margriet de Moor.

Also by Cees Nooteboom in English translation

FICTION

Rituals

In the Dutch Mountains

Philip and the Others

The Following Story

The Knight Has Died

A Song of Truth and Semblance

Mokusei

All Souls' Day

Lost Paradise

NON-FICTION

Roads to Santiago

Nomad's Hotel

Roads to Berlin

POETRY

Self-portrait of an Other

"Nooteboom's characters gaze with melancholy and astonishment at a lost moment now crystallised or gone to seed . . . The stories are composed and connected with an emphasis on theme rather than plot – each one an eddy of memory revolving and rippling with thoughts of past loves and inexorable deaths"

GALEN O'HANLON, *T.L.S.*

"One of the most remarkable writers of our time . . . The outstanding characteristic of his writing is its elegant intelligence . . . Nooteboom forces his readers to reflect on what is being said, and to take up their part in the work: for him, literature is a collaborative effort"

ALBERTO MANGUEL, *Guardian*

"Nooteboom's short novels are exquisite toys for the broken-hearted, erudite tales that revolve around themes of loss and despair but are never less than playful"   JONATHAN GIBBS, *Independent*

Cees Nooteboom

THE FOXES COME
AT NIGHT

Translated from the Dutch by
Ina Rilke

MACLEHOSE PRESS
QUERCUS · LONDON

First published in the Netherlands as 's Nachts Komen de Vossen
by De Bezige Bij, Amsterdam, 2009

First published in Great Britain in 2011 by MacLehose Press

This paperback edition published in 2013 by
MacLehose Press
an imprint of Quercus
55 Baker Street
7th Floor, South Block
London W1U 8EW

This book was published with the support of
the Dutch Foundation for Literature

ISBN (Paperback) 978 1 84916 557 0
ISBN (Ebook) 978 0 85705 168 4

2 4 6 8 10 9 7 5 3 1

Designed and typeset in Albertina by Libanus Press, Marlborough
Printed and bound in Great Britain by Clays Ltd, St Ives plc

CONTENTS

"You might have got yourself a story," I said.
"Sure. But up here we're just people."

Raymond Chandler, *The Lady in the Lake*

Gondolas

Gondolas are atavistic. Where he had read that he did not know, nor did he wish to think about it now for fear of losing the pathos of the moment. A low sun, the black, bird-like shape of a gondola on the misty lagoon, the squat mooring posts like a solitary phalanx of soldiers vanishing into the distance on a mission of death and destruction, and him standing motionless on the Riva degli Schiavoni holding a snapshot, yellowed and half-torn – how was that for pathos? It was roughly here that their gondola had arrived, and there, by those steps, or the next ones a bit closer to the half-submerged statue of the executed partisan woman, that they had disembarked. The weather had been much like this, you could still tell from the snapshot. They had been sitting on the steps when a young officer appeared, pointing to a sign and telling them the place was reserved for the water police. All he had to do now was locate the sign, which should not be too difficult.

And if I find it, what then? Then I'll be standing on the very same spot where I stood forty years ago, and what of it? He shrugged, as though someone else were putting the question. So nothing. And that, he thought, was the whole point.

He had agreed to write a piece about the show at the Palazzo Grassi for the sole purpose of undertaking this curious pilgrimage. Where to? To a phantom, no, not even that, to an absence. He had found the very steps quite easily. They were still in use as a mooring place for the police. Eternal cities tend not to change too much, and the sign was still there, fixed to the brickwork on the side. Newly painted, though. He sat down on the top step. The youthful *carabiniere* from back then would have long since been pensioned off, but even if he had stayed young in the intervening forty years he would not have recognized the elderly man sitting there now. The snapshot had been taken by an unknown bystander, who had posted himself with his back to the lagoon some distance away. An angle of thirty degrees, so that the Doge's Palace would be in the picture. Peering closely, he marvelled at its falsity. Not only could a photograph conjure up people who were dead, it could also confront you with a hopelessly outdated version of yourself, in this case a long-haired stranger whose appearance had once been so much of the period that it gave the scene the stale aroma of a long-buried past.

The mere fact of being in possession of the same body – that was the true marvel. But of course it was not the same body. The person in possession of the body still went by the same name, that was as much as you could say.

What that snapshot really conveyed, he reflected, more as a statement of fact than out of a sense of tragedy or self-pity, was that it was time he started thinking about his own exit. He had been sitting to her left. She had tilted her laughing face to the unknown photographer, tossed her red hair from her forehead and arched her back against the wall, half-obscuring the sign. He looked down at the greyish water eddying around the lower steps. How extraordinary that things should still be the same! The water, the cormorant-shaped gondolas, the marble step on which he sat. It is just us making our exit, he thought, we leave the décor of our lives behind. He ran his hand over the pitted stone surface beside him, as though trying to feel her absence. He was aware that every thought entering the mind under these circumstances would be a cliché, but these riddles had never been solved. By reality and perfection I mean the same thing – this time he knew the origin of the statement. Whether Hegel was alluding to a situation such as the present one was doubtful, and yet it seemed so apt. He felt strangely cheered by the notion that things just happened to be the way they were, that it was impossible to conceive of them rationally at all. Death was a natural given, but it was accompanied by such abysmal sorrow at times that you were almost ready to descend into the abyss yourself, and thereby surrender to the perfect reality of the riddle.

The beginning had been quite straightforward. A Greek island, a house belonging to friends of friends, lent to him out of pity on account of his recent divorce. Unused to being alone, hungry for female company. A paved walkway along the shore peopled by all those walking, strolling women whom he longed to accost but did not dare, in case they laughed and thought him an idiot. "Ankatzen" was what his friend Wintrop used to call "making a pass". Nothing wrong with the expression, but he had never been good at it. What was that line from Lucebert's poem again? Evenings spent wandering past womanly ships. That bit was true, at least. There and back, there and back, ambling, dawdling, looking. Hydra, fishing boats, white in the darkening night, bobbing gently in the light of tall sodium lamps on the quay. Swallows, cypresses – or was he imagining things? Did they have sodium lighting in those days? But why should his memory have to be accurate? Make it yellow lamplight, hear an owl, see the dark shapes of pine trees. The only certainty is the sea softly lapping the quayside. All the rest is replaceable, the arsenal of props whereby memories are furnished.

*

There had been no resemblance to a ship when she came past. Or perhaps there had: some super-light craft with a single sail, the kind that skims the surface. He must have looked ridiculous, leaping to his feet on the quay and raising his hand like a policeman stopping traffic. And that was in fact what he had said, STOP! Even now he felt a twinge of embarrassment, for all that they had joked about it later, in California, when everything was long over. She had been so startled that she stopped in her tracks. Curiously, he couldn't remember whether she had gone with him that first evening. They had talked for a long time in a harbour café. She was American, her name Italian. Sixteen, eighteen? He had wanted to ask but had not dared. He had already noticed the black markings on her hands and arms, zodiac signs, not tattooed as they would have been today, but inked on her sun-tanned skin. When he asked her about them she said oh, but I'm a witch. That was another thing they had laughed about afterwards, but he still had her letters from those days, lengthy tirades about magic and sorcery, exalted ramblings he was unable to take seriously but found intriguing all the same. They were in tune with the times, but even more so with the red hair, the slate-grey eyes, the astonishingly deep, slightly hoarse tone of voice. In the days that followed she had slept at the big white house. But not with him. That was the deal. She suffered him to caress her, averting her face, and then dropped off to sleep with oblivious, animal abandon. He had felt a bit silly and *de trop*, but had found her trust touching. Better to have company than love, he had noted in his diary. Later on he had thrown the diary away, something he now regretted, but he could still remember jotting down those words. That had been a few days before everything changed. Perhaps he was only imagining it, but he seemed to remember her pointing to one of the strange markings on her body when she made that remark about the moment being auspicious. Something to do with planets being in alignment, the kind of thing he already dismissed as nonsense back then.

In her lovemaking she had been at once coy and childlike; those were the words he had come up with for want of anything better. "Coy" had never sounded quite right, there was something purposeful and possibly even calculating about it, but those were not the right terms either. He had been aroused by the hint of forbidden games in her affect-ations of innocence, as though she were challenging him for having underage sex, an experience quite new to him then and not repeated since.

He headed back to town. The Piero della Francesca exhibition had deeply affected him. Why he should see a parallel there with an affair several decades ago was unclear, maybe it was just that his mind was at once occupied with the artist and the recollection, or that there was some meaning to those paintings that was impossible to pinpoint, which could also be said of the short weeks they had been together. She could hardly be described as mysterious, her talk of sorcery was childish babble, but somehow the absence he now felt at his side reminded him of the hieratic figures in these paintings. You stood before them yearning to penetrate their world, but it was a world to which there was no access. He was at a loss how to write his article, and no less confounded by his feelings about the remembered episode.

They had taken a train, back then, right across Greece to Yugoslavia. He could summon little of the journey apart from shabby hotel rooms and a halo of red hair on a pillow. A night in Belgrade, a sort of beer garden, where they were plied with slivovitz by a party of revellers who tossed their emptied glasses over their shoulders onto the gravel. Then they arrived in Venice. He had forgotten which hotel, but not where the snapshot had been taken. He turned and retraced his steps.

It was intolerable, really, how someone could simply vanish from your life. What you needed was a hundredfold parallel lives, that would only be fair. Farewell at the railway station, stepping out on to the Fondamenta Santa Lucia, alone again, a man in a crowd having just witnessed a person's re-engulfment by the world at large, a slender arm waving from a compartment window, a train vanishing over the illuminated rectangle of the Ponte della Ferrovia, and then nothing. In the present of forty years on he returned to his hotel room and leafed through the exhibition catalogue. How absurd, to look for a connection with Piero della Francesca.

What sort of girl had she been? A flower child of the '60s, whereas he had been lonely, all too ready to fall in love and lap up her claims about planets and stars interfering with their fortunes. As if celestial bodies had nothing better to do!

But at night, on the waterfront, with her voice meandering on about Saturn and Pluto as if they were animate beings in space, spinning the threads along which the lives of a seventeen-year-old from Mills Valley and a freelance art journalist from Amsterdam would take their course, he had felt a curious sense of captivation, not because of what she was saying, but because of the way her slate-grey eyes seemed to light up in the dark.

Love was the need for love, that much at least he had understood. The intentions of an assortment of lifeless gases and ice balls in outer space were simply a fable people told themselves in a desperate bid to replace other, outmoded fables, and if you could not handle that you had no business waylaying random passers-by.

Back in his empty apartment in Amsterdam he had waited for news from her, letters written in an unaesthetic, almost naive American hand, margins splattered with zodiacs and Sicilian signs to ward off the evil eye, and he wondered what on earth he had written in reply. He no longer knew which of them had stopped writing, but he had a clear memory of the excitement he had felt, a good twenty years on, at receiving a letter written in the old familiar scrawl. She had read his essay on Jacoba van Heemskerck, she had seen it in the catalogue of a San Francisco exhibition devoted to spiritual art. She had been through a lot, she reported. Marriage, divorce, two sons, and she had taken up painting. Some of her pictures might even remind him of Jacoba van Heemskerck. She had enclosed two photographs, compositions of nebulous planes in shades that reminded him of the colour of her eyes, grey with a dusting of highlights. Art for a meditation centre. Things had not gone well for her, but Buddhism had been a great help. She had been in contact with a monastery nearby, where she had found solace, and which she would have joined had it not been for her sons. She had thought of him often. And there must surely be some affinity of the soul that had moved him to write about Jacoba's work, which was virtually unknown in the States, although she had found it a source of inspiration and especially of consolation because of all the bad stuff that had happened in her life, the details of which she would spare him. She hoped her letter would reach him, and believed her visit to the exhibition to have been a sign. Was it not strange how people you once knew just dropped off the planet? That you did not even know whether a particular person was still alive, despite having travelled together and shared the same experiences? She had been so young at the time, a child really, living in a sort of dream, what with the old house on Hydra and that long train ride through parched landscapes, and finally Venice, where she hoped to return some day. She had talked a load of nonsense back then, goodness knows, but he had respected her the way she was, and she was grateful for that because things could easily have been different. She was not sure he would understand what she meant, but what she was trying to say was that he had not taken advantage of her. He was not to think she was after anything, it was just that finding someone among the billions of people on earth was a miracle in its own right. Neither was he to feel obliged to reply to her letter, of course, but she would love to hear how he was getting on.

Not very well, would have been the honest answer. That was not what he would reply, nor would he tell her the essay on Jacoba van Heemskerck was just another assignment, that he considered her work worthy but also rather vapid, and that as far as he was concerned the renewed interest in her was due to the general upsurge in airy-fairyness, a fashion of which she had in fact been a precursor. Fine colouring, possibly even a dynamism akin to that of Kandinsky, but not his thing. The sort of art that had arisen as a reaction to the nineteenth century, a period he disliked intensely. Instead, he told her he was writing an academic thesis on Piero della Francesca. Was she familiar with that artist? And yes, he was glad she had got in touch. What would it be like to meet again? He still had that snapshot of her on the Riva degli Schiavoni sitting on a bollard, had he ever sent her a copy? He could not remember. And dismissing the whole nineteenth century like that was unfair, really, considering that Flaubert, Stendhal and Balzac did wage war on the old-world torpor that had stifled so many hopes and expectations, but he needed only to look at their daguerreotype likenesses, at the stiffness resulting from lengthy exposure times, to know how much he would have hated being confined in the antechamber of modernism. That snapshot! A girl on an outsize bollard, substantial enough to provide moorage for an ocean liner. A flimsy dress with a dash of purple, and above it the ephemeral features of a human being, transitory as dust. A madonna by Bellini, but he had not told her that, the art historian must always beware of comparison. And yet, even without the child she had been a madonna. The same doom-laden shadow on the left side of her face, the inward-looking eyes that had seen the future tragedy of the child on her knee a hundred times over, and then the child itself, a wizened sage who knew that his mother's cherishing hand would not be shielding him in the hour of his death.

He had already made up his mind before he reached the end of her letter. He would go and visit her, and he did. A pointless exercise, one of his friends had called it, but he had thought otherwise. It was unfinished business, and it needed finishing.

A trip to America was part of the process, someone waiting for him at the airport in San Francisco, a woman whose appearance told him how much he himself had aged. People were fantastic. They should be decorated again and again. The split-second appraisal, the mental snapshot of extreme, unmentionable sharpness. Lines about the eyes, hair still flaming red but with an overlying haze, imprints of time giving rise to a sudden sense of camaraderie, possibly even of tenderness. There was more love there than before, he could tell right away, a love he would do nothing with, that too he could tell. The vulnerability had increased. A wooden house, suburb of a suburb, watercolours in the Rudolf Steiner mode, art he had never had a liking for, a fact he would have mentioned in the past but now found surprisingly easy to conceal. You are still a dreamer, he had said, and she had been true to her old self, claiming it was Saturn she had to thank for her pastel creations. A week of utmost ecstasy, night after night of feeling the power, and when it was all over she had felt emptier than ever before, empty, but happy.

Not long after that she had been to see the exhibition, where she received the sign telling her to contact him. But she had never thought he would make the journey.

"Women's aftercare" was the phrase that entered his mind. He had come to finish something.

Finishing was not the same as closure. There was yet an opening. Usually that was all: there had been an episode, then there was distance, and time, wear and tear, and forgetting. A thought now and then, a vague recollection, that was normal, that was the way things went, unless you took some sort of action. There was still something missing, a form of verification, of saying goodbye. Things needed rounding off, not just for your own sake, but also for the other person's, unless they did not care of course. That was why he had gone to Mills Valley. And now that she was dead, that was why he was here, in Venice.

Had she not mentioned something in her letter about hard times? About bad stuff happening in her life? Yes, but she did not want to talk about that now.

She suggested going to the beach for a stroll. The weather was good, a bit blustery, but that was fitting enough. Or was he too tired? No, he would enjoy a walk, good to feel the wind on his face. No swimming, though, on account of the cold current, not to mention the rip tides; it was a beautiful place, but dangerous. And indeed it was. Marin County, McClure's Beach, the long road downhill, grassland on either side with herds of massive elk, a protected species. Rutting season, you can hear them bugle sometimes, when they charge each other with those huge antlers. Down below all was pounding surf, walls of rushing water, sandpipers tracing minimal alphabets in the sand as they scurried ahead of the waves. The sustained roar of a pipe organ, just the place to finish a story that had begun twenty years earlier. Like shouting into the wind.

Thoughts of fate and doom do not accord with the mainland palette, not with the infantile colours worn by the elderly, not with the pastel shades of the clapboard houses, not with paintings imitating those of a Dutch woman artist from the heyday of anthroposophy. So you head for the mighty ocean, where you can hurl your words into the wind. A woman's voice vying with the surf, lamenting a runaway poet, a child turned drug addict, a disease with an inbuilt time bomb, *but I have learnt acceptance.*

A bit much, don't you think, she said later in the car. That was the phrase that had accompanied him to Venice: a bit much. They had written to each other a few more times, but his questions regarding her health she had ignored. The planets and stars were now more than ever her companions, she had written, she had the feeling she would be lifted up. She had dedicated to him one of her watercolour paintings, which he would receive in due course. He was not to feel sorry for her, she had just returned from the beach, the sunset had been awesome, with a long ribbon of red coming straight to the sand at her feet, so she could have walked on the water straight to the horizon.

After a few weeks he received the watercolour, which he had seen in her home, and which he would not put up on his wall. He also received the letters he had sent in the final months, and those of twenty years before, which he now dropped, unread, into the lagoon. That's what dustbins are for, a voice said behind him. He did not answer, and watched as the crumpled sheets drifted away on the ashy, evening-coloured water, until a gondola came by and they were gone.

Thunderstorm

I am my own barometer, he said as they stood peering at the barometer. I can feel it in my skeleton. Anyone else would have said "in my bones", but Rudolf said skeleton, because he knew that it would irritate Rosita. He also knew why she would be irritated; which made it worse. She had a literal mind and consequently visualized a skeleton, and found it distasteful. The days of Vanitas paintings are over, she said, nor do people keep skulls on their desks anymore. If you had said that an hour ago I wouldn't have fucked with you, it's no fun having a skeleton on top of you. She imagined rattling ribcages, grinning skulls. You're such a jerk sometimes. And only because the weather is changing. He made no comment, because it was true, both accusations were. Summer had come to an abrupt end, with castles of grey clouds, the white of the Spanish houses suddenly dingy, the garden flooded, because when the rain came it did so with a vengeance, in buckets. As did the attendant melancholy. Doors that had been left open all summer had now to be closed, the long walks along the shore had to be taken earlier in the day, and there was a dark hole between sundown and the Spanish dinner hour. That meant an earlier drink in a bar, or else huddling with a book by an electric fire in a house that had suddenly lost its charm. Exasperatingly, none of this bothered her in the least. Come to that, she did not seem bothered by anything. Not by sleeplessness, not by boredom. She simply withdrew to her study, in apparent contentment. How anyone could be content to spend years on end researching the history of the Dutch labour movement was a mystery to him. Everything she mentioned about the protagonists, from Domela Nieuwenhuis up to and including Henriette Roland Holst, filled him with deep suspicion. People with double-barrelled names, all of them, brimming with good intentions towards the exploited masses. A century had gone by since then, and the to-be-uplifted class of once upon a time is now standing on a ladder tattoo'd like a Maori, his radio turned up full blast, painting the house next door. Blaring voices, oily disc jockeys, and new soap stars with vulgar accents for the whole run of the season. If only the high-minded Gorters and Van Eedens could come back and see what it's like now, he would say, they would get the fright of their lives. Finally succeeded, the dictatorship of the proletariat, art for the people. I see the working classes dancing in silver rows on the edge of the ocean . . . the poet Herman Gorter, I believe. And it has worked, too – in the disco at Torremolinos. Her usual response would be to start humming softly, which he never knew whether to take for an expression of contempt or of pity. A faint, high, twittering sound, a bit like a bird poised to fly up and away.

But she had no intention of taking flight. I bought into you, with all your moaning and groaning, she had declared during one of his rare displays of remorse. She had fallen for a man who carved statues out of wood, who was his own barometer, and who was highly susceptible to solar dearth. Once the sun was gone it became necessary to tap secret reservoirs and contrive ways to ward off all-encompassing gloom. Night and winter were his natural enemies. The wood lay untouched in his studio, no carved dream-figures materialized, galleries were left in the lurch. At such times he was a ship adrift in an ocean of darkness. She sensed that her own equanimity grated on him, but she also knew that her stoicism in the face of what he termed his black gall was what kept him going in times of habituation to the darker seasons. The best strategy was to confront it head on.

Shall we go to San Hilario?

He shrugged. San Hilario was a good thirty kilometres away. The drive there passed through a fairly wild landscape. There was a little bay with a beach they had known when it was still pristine, but a developer had since gone and built a hotel. Not far from there, on the sea front, was an old café where they served simple food, what the Spanish call a *chiringuito*. White-painted interior, plastic tables, a large paved terrace, aluminium chairs that made a squeaky scraping sound when shifted. In this dark weather the strip lights would already be switched on. Neon helped, she had learnt from experience, but she did not mention that. A cool fake sun, long, white and thin; a placebo that worked.

It was the end of the season, hence no tourists to speak of. On the way there was an almighty thunderstorm. The clouds had become the colour of lead, heavy masses lowering menacingly over the green of the oleasters. The land lit up eerily, the first flash of lightning. The ensuing sharp, dry thunderclap was followed by hailstones gusting wildly against the car, drumming on the roof. She glanced sideways, knowing he would be glad of the storm. There ought to be a language to describe every type of cloud, he had remarked one day. Belgian bluestone, chalk, slate, goose-down, treacherous grit. She knew he wanted to stop the car and go out into the storm. Anything for a bit of drama. What I want is the unbridled forces of nature, was how he described it. And he was getting his way, as usual. She had difficulty keeping the small Seat on the road. A solitary biker got off his machine and stood on the verge for a long moment like a statue, etched in the landscape by the lightning. The parking lot next to the café was as good as empty. When she got out she stepped into ankle-deep water. As they made a dash for the sheltered terrace they heard the roar of the surf, aggravated by the high-pitched howl of the wind. The expanse of grey sea merged with the grey of the sky; the islet just off shore was scarcely visible.

Five people at an outdoor café: two women in raincoats a bit further off, a solitary black man in a yellow shirt trying to read, a couple at a table nearby. Enough for a film.

That was what Rudolf said. She was used to him seeing things as if he were watching a film. Usually she agreed with him. And in this case the ingredients were all there. Unity of time, place, action. Drama enough with that storm raging, and by the look of the couple at the next table they were having a blazing, bottled-up row. You could tell before even a word had been exchanged. The woman was good-looking. Shoes, blouse, raincoat, everything she wore was white, and in addition her pale lipstick was almost fluorescent, as if she had chosen it to match the weather. She did not seem to feel the cold. He did, he sat hunched over in his red windcheater, scowling at the ground, a large glass of brandy in his hand. Rosita did not think the woman looked much like her, but the couple did seem to mirror her own marriage, which she found somewhat disconcerting. She did not mention it aloud, not least because her strategy was proving effective: Rudolf's moroseness had lifted, even as the storm gathered force. As though he were being recharged by the electricity out of doors. She saw him observing the woman as she attempted to photograph the lightning with a small digital camera.

She could tell from his expression that his mind was on things sculptural, which would no doubt materialize at some later stage. She was not sure whether you could say that lips frowned, but that was what he was doing in her view, a weird, eager, tense pursing of the lips while registering every movement of the camera, which the woman in white kept aiming at the lightning. Such lightning! In those regions thunderstorms were a phenomenon apart. Long streaks of blinding whiteness, sometimes several at a time, and the ever louder crashes of the approaching thunder.

Don't be so stupid, the man in the windcheater growled in German, so loudly that you knew he assumed no-one would understand. Rosita had ordered in Spanish, and could pass for a local anyway. The woman took another photograph, and this time she did seem to have captured the lightning. *Arschloch. Du bist wirklich ein Arschloch.* She sounded calm and matter-of-fact, almost like a tour guide.

Let me be or go back to the hotel. I'll carry on doing this

as long as I . . . the rest of her sentence was drowned in a thunderclap so close that the whole terrace shook.

There's no way you'll get that into your picture, the man said.

With the next crash the lights went out. All you could see during subsequent flashes was the wicker fence dividing the terrace from the slope down to the sand. That and the surf pounding the beach. Evidently the woman was trying again to take a photograph of the electric scrawl shooting across the horizon, for they could hear the nervous beep of her camera and see a tremulous pinprick of red light. In the final moments before the lights came on again the man must have knocked the camera from her grasp: it lay in a large puddle on the edge of the terrace. The woman slapped him across the face and said once more the word, underscored this time by the squeaky scrape of the aluminium chair as the man jumped to his feet, still holding his glass. He moved stiffly away, like a robot programmed to head for the steps leading down to the beach. The waiter came running from his post by the window inside the café, but the black man was already sprinting to the steps, which the German was slowly descending. What Rosita would never forget was the ghastly alternation of light and dark, the man with the glass vanishing repeatedly, as though engulfed by successive waves of darkness. Each time they saw him he was a pace nearer the sea, his robotic gait unchanged.

He's going to sink himself, said Rudolf, but it did not come to that.

When the lightning struck it was as though he were being doused with electricity. Liquid sparks, white light streaking down the dark outline of his body. Even above the roar of the surf they could hear him shriek, a cry of shattered words dissolving into the woman's screaming and a new crash of thunder. They saw the waiter and the black man standing over the victim's sprawled body, not daring to touch. But that was not until later, after the arrival of an ambulance, sirens pulverizing the night. Statements were taken by the police, the woman whimpering throughout, but no-one mentioned the quarrel, as though by general consent. Not until their names and addresses had been noted down were they were allowed to leave. When they made their way to the car through the mud, the sky in the distance was still scribbled with electricity, but the thunder had passed out of earshot, the wind had dropped. Only the rain was still there, soft but intense.

The road had become a torrent, here and there they had to swerve to avoid broken branches.

Rudolf had put on a C.D. of choral music by Kurtág, which

he often played in his studio. It was not Rosita's favourite kind of music. Thin, high voices ascending to great heights, hallowed sounds from behind the closed door of his studio, sounds that excluded her. But at the same time they signalled to her that he was back at work. Those voices are my guides, he had once remarked. She had tried to imagine what it was like for him to listen to those tones spinning themselves out so strangely, as if they were sustained until the end of the breath and then tumbled over each other in a whirl of staccato repetitions. Sometimes it made her think of a distant crowd of people debating a terrible secret, the nub of which eluded her, due to that closed door. Now, in the car, those voices somehow seemed to belong to the scene they had just witnessed. In her mind's eye she saw the woman, suddenly subdued, being led to the ambulance by two paramedics, who sat her down on a low seat beside the human shape covered by a sheet. It was only a couple of hours since she had seen the mirror image. She shivered, and glanced sidelong at the closed expression on the face next to her. The music now made her think of war between the sexes, with the women's voices like battle cries. She shivered, realizing that she had never seen anyone die before.

As a doornail, Rudolf had replied to her question whether the man was dead; ten electric chairs, you could smell the sizzle of flesh, you were burnt to a crisp.

he often played in his studio. It was not Rosita's favourite

*

The road was deserted. The story would be splashed across the local newspapers the following day, and people would flock to see where it had taken place. Nothing much happened on the island, road accidents made the headlines. He waved his hand abruptly, saying could you stop the car a moment.

He always noticed things before she did, she was used to that. She knew he would fetch out the small saw he kept in the boot in case he came across any interesting piece of wood. She watched him in the rear-view mirror as he walked back some way along the verge until he vanished among the trees. He had taken the big torch, she could still see the occasional flash of tree trunks. She turned the music down and listened to the patter of the rain vying with the windscreen wipers, tick-tack, tick-tack. Then she heard him call her name. She switched on the blink lights and stepped out of the car. He was standing by a fallen tree uprooted by the storm, and asked her to hold the torch for him. In the yellow beam the exposed clump at the base resembled the head of a giant medusa, with fibrous roots like huge dreadlocks clotted with earth and stones. She felt threatened by all those tentacles, and involuntarily took a step back. Don't, he said. Come closer. He sounded severe, as he always did when his mind was focused. He brushed away the loose, reddish-brown earth and began to saw at one of the roots, a crooked, gnarly length of wood that seemed to be alive, which of course it was.

He held it up in the torchlight. There was a strange angle to it, like a reclining figure with drawn-up knees.

It looks like a foetus, she said, but he said nothing, just gave her one of those looks that told her she had said something she shouldn't have. They made their way back to the car in silence, stowed the piece of wood in the boot. He was humming to himself, and forgot to turn up the music. For a long while she maintained her silence, but then she asked anyway.

What do you think it's like, being struck by lightning? Are you killed outright?

No, not necessarily. But the voltage you get is massive. Your body is seventy per cent water, so you evaporate, really. The only resistance comes from the bones. He was making it up.

You don't really know, do you?

No, I don't, he said, but he was dead alright. Burnt. His face was all carbonized. Water conducts, and it was raining.

Neither of them spoke after that. On their return he went straight to his studio.

She heard him scraping the piece of tree root. The following morning she saw that he had propped it against the hearth. Its crookedness seemed to suggest that it was in pain, as if some mighty force had twisted it into an unnatural shape. Yet it had been nature at work.

Not for burning, he said, let it dry. In the light of morning she could see what it would become.

For a moment, when the woman had resumed taking photographs, the man's eyes had met hers. Light blue eyes. He had wanted to say something to her, she thought, but he had not. She, for her part, had smiled and briefly lifted her hand.

She did not buy the newspaper the following day. To not have a name.

Heinz

"What an empty episode!" said Eliza. "It seems to have no meaning."

"It has none," said Sir Robert. "So we will not give it one. We will not pretend that something has happened when nothing has."

Ivy Compton-Burnett, *The Last and the First*

1

First a round of deception. I am looking at a photograph of a group of people, which includes me. Next I have to pretend not to know who any of them are. Then what do I see? No, I must redouble the deception. From where I am sitting now, writing this, I can see a field and a narrow provincial road bearing to the left. The asphalt is wet. It is winter, though not snowy, which is unusual for this time of year. The branches are bare. Beeches, a dead pine tree, a pond. There's supposed to be a grave somewhere around there, but it is unmarked. Beyond that a second field, and a third. The ground is soggy, rain-soaked, as I know from my walks. In the far distance a skreeper of black woodland.

"Skreeper" may not be in the dictionary, but it goes rather well with deception.

Language is something you inherit, it's never just you doing the talking, which helps when you're pretending. In clear weather I'd be able to see the Alps, in which case the pretence would be more blatant, as there's no trace of a mountain in the picture before me. I stare at the gathering. They – I must stick to "they" for now, "we" does not come into it till later – are standing in a Mediterranean landscape. A long way away both in distance and in time. A windblown bunch, dressed for the outdoors. Five men, two women, half a white dog. Had the photograph been one centimetre larger you would have known whether the left ear of the dog was tipped with black. Ramshackle farm cart in the background. What sort of a game is this, pretending not to know who the people are? Is that really the way I might be able to solve their riddles? Just by looking? Or am I trying to see them as strangers precisely because I know plenty already? They have all lived for fifty years or so, that much is obvious. Poverty is not their problem, that too is obvious. Comfortable class, country clothes.

They may be going out hunting later, or have horses to see to. Anyone coming across this snapshot today, or fifty years from now – what would they be thinking? In the case of today, would his or her curiosity be aroused, would she be interested in the men, would he find the women attractive? In fifty years' time the questions will be different. The people in it will have been relegated to the realm of the dead, or to the decrepitude of old age, by which time observing the image will have become a melancholy exercise, fleeting and inconsequential. The dead have few rights. So for now I shall let them live, and pretend the image is a current one, depicting a present in which those seven people are opposite an invisible photographer, male or female. Only one of them is laughing: the man in the cap. The others have a hint of a smile about the lips, that's all. Whether the person taking the photograph, male or female, is a friend is impossible to say, although it seems likely, since no-one is posing. They just happen to be standing there, more or less in a straight line, facing the camera. Within two seconds their line will break up as they resume their various conversations. Right then, scrivener, what are you getting at? Only if you had Alzheimer's would you no longer know who those people are. Yes, it's you I'm talking to. You are one of the seven. Two of the men you don't remember, which leaves four people, including the one I am devoting this story to, since he's the only one who's dead. Why all the mystery? Am I beefing it all up into something it never was? Drama in novels or films exists thanks to the denial of duration, since it can be compressed into a few evenings of reading or an hour or two of viewing. Things happen in the real world which you can call dramas, and yet, if you want to turn them into art you have no choice but to converge and compress. Length was a virtue in the nineteenth century: take Stendhal, take Trollope. But we can no longer digest such lengths any more, our attention span has shrunk. Our chaos makes for stories lacking in form and clarity. In a good story the temporal aspect is both dispensed with and manifest. In a photograph the aspect of absence plays a significant role, but just how significant is impossible to tell. I mean, if you have never met the people in the photo, you can't begin to know who is absent. That is the difference. Heinz stands next to his wife, but his first wife is not there. Heinz? Fourth from the left and fourth from the right. Not counting the dog, he occupies the exact centre. German name, but not a German. Central figure. Of the group, and of this story. So I have not kept up the pretence for very long – of course I know who they are. So why make all this effort? Can I tell this at the end?

2

The Ligurian coast. Anyone who has read Eugenio Montale's *Ossi di sepia* knows what that means. Cuttlefish bone. Beyond the coastal decay stretches a hinterland of classical allure, close your eyes and you will see a Roman legion march past, en route to Gaul, to us. Cuttlefish belong to the mollusc family, but what they leave behind when they die is neither snail-shell nor sea-shell, it is a bone: strange, chalky-looking, white and oval, not solid but delicate, something you used to see in canary cages. Not as food, I believe, but more something for the songsters to sharpen their beaks on. To Montale it evidently symbolized his homeland, and he had a point. A calcareous residue of life, rocky substrate, friable sandstone, a land of cypress and holm oak, cactus and lemon tree. Age-old farmhouses dotted about, like the one we stood before on that day, God knows what year – keeping track of time has never been my forte. The man in the cap was the salesman, all smiles, not that it did him any good. Nobody was buying. He was the only Italian in our group, the others were English, except for myself and another Dutchman, by the name of Heinz. None of us lived in the town on the coast, our homes were out in the ancient villages and surrounding hills. At this juncture I will have to describe the photograph, of course, but first a word of warning. When do things become a drama? There is the unity of time, place and action, of course, that time-honoured straitjacket of stagecraft. If that is what you expect, you are in for a disappointment. Drama enough, but no straitjacket, and consequently no art. No culmination, no *dénouement*. The last three actors were Heinz, a pigeon, and death. I was an extra, as usual, and Molly was hiding in the wings. But they took their time, the curtain had long since fallen, the audience departed. Everything took too long. Heinz was alone with his play, as were Philip and Andrea, standing at either end of the group, unless you count the salesman. Not by accident, not by chance. Now then, from left to right. The salesman, the laughing man in the cap. We can cross him out. Then come the actual *personae*. *Non dramatis*. The first is Andrea. From the feet up: white running shoes, narrow black trousers, long white T-shirt, and a jacket made of white knobbly wool, a sort of white astrakhan, if such a thing exists. Fake fur perhaps, you cannot tell. She is one of those women on whom fake looks real. Her stance strikes me as equestrian, but perhaps that is only because I know she rides. There was a time when I was in love with her, we tried to make a go of it, but it didn't work. A daily dose of *The Sun*, nothing but horses for the rest. That was what attracted me in the first place, but she wouldn't believe me when I told her. *In your secret heart you're an arrogant intellectual, you're laughing at me.* Untrue, that, but I couldn't convince her. Have you ever seen a woman canter over the hills in the twilight? Scandal sheets are no match for atavism. Slovenian nobility, but that is not something one mentions if one is English. Too silly. Father an anti-Semite and a great horseman, fled from Tito, married money in England. To the right of her two metres of nothing, some flour sacks leaning against the wall, then the nameless yachtsman who just happened to be there that day. Open, affable expression. No need for a coat, accustomed to the cold at sea. Then Heinz. Large, burly. It was on account of him that I wanted to pretend they were all strangers, curious as I was about the possibility of detecting signs of his future downfall. Try as I might, though, there was nothing to be seen, not now, let alone fifty years hence. No sign either of what I already knew about him back then. A big man in a black roll-neck, open jacket, rumpled trousers, wrong shoes, the antithesis of the person at his side, his wife. Molly. Her English resembles that of Philip and Andrea, not Oxford, something more redolent of Jags, cricket and horses, but also of tabloids with screaming headlines and boobs on page three. Posh, no books, that just about sums it up. Expats, but home is only a two-hour flight away and the language is everywhere, unlike the taxman. Molly wears sunglasses with a white frame. With some English women you can be sure you will never see their real faces. *Tous les anglais sont fous par nature ou par ton*, as Chateaubriand said from the grave, and that counts for the women too.

Loosely draped white scarf, bright blonde hair, three-quarter-length tweed coat. Last time I saw her, a stooped old lady with a small dog on a country road, she didn't recognize me. Here I stand beside her, a former edition of my chameleonic self. The spot where my elbow now rests on the

German table would be where my wife stood, aiming her camera. I.e. the photographer was female. Following the lines of perspective with my gaze I can see exactly where her feet were planted on the smooth, sandy-coloured rocks. I too wear a loosely tied scarf. After all this time I still know which one it was, green with a small tartan pattern. On our epic journey from nothing to nowhere we leave behind an endless trail of garments. I feel a pang of nostalgia for certain items sometimes, which is all the more reason not to dwell on old photographs. Next to me is Philip. Suede shoes, quilted jacket, hair – already greying – ruffled by the breeze. He has the stentorian voice of his father, who once listed all the battles he had missed in the war, for my benefit: Monte Cassino, too much gin and a nasty fall over a tent-peg; El Alamein, woken too late by his batman; Jerusalem, command over a female regiment. Philip had dabbled in real estate, along with Heinz. Now divorced from Andrea on account of the horses. *Time only for those goddam horses. Out in the morning at six. Never at home.*

But the story is not about Philip and Andrea. It is about Heinz.

3

Of all the ranks the Dutch Ministry of Foreign Affairs can bestow, that of honorary vice-consul is surely the lowest. Honorary means no pay, and vice means there's likely to be another person in charge whose title is of the full variety, but in Heinz's case that did not apply. He had no superior, which was just as well. Every halfway-decent port in a region frequented by Dutch nationals needs a consulate. Dutch people abroad die, get arrested, crash their cars, lose their money or their passports or both, in which cases the long arm of the fatherland must be able to reach over the frontiers to succour those in need. In exchange the honorary consul, usually a local businessman with barely a smattering of Dutch, is entitled to display the Netherlands royal coat of arms on the façade of his house, which affords him considerable local prestige. A pair of golden lions clawing at each other with heraldic tongues protruding from gaping maws are good for business, which is generally conducted on the same premises. *Je maintiendrai*, it says in likewise golden lettering on that tall, oval shield, the royal motto Heinz was wont to translate as "I shall keep up standards", a notion that, along with a knowledge of French, is fast disappearing from the idiom of the new generations. *Maîtresses*, kept women, concubines, all of them extinct, traded in for the devalued term "girlfriend", which was not to say that Heinz eschewed such a relationship. For that he had his secretary, who would on occasion service him under his desk. Sigismonda, a jolly forty-eight-year-old whose horsey features, as he referred to them, he found endearing. He was of a cheery disposition, which was not something one would expect of someone going by the name of Heinz Maximilian. That was the trouble with having an Austrian mother, he would say, but I can be happy to have escaped being an Adolf.

I take another long look at the photograph. A cheerful soul. But was he? What about the melancholy, what about the alcohol?

But that was the whole point, that irresistible combination, the reason I still think of him today. That's what I meant by "no *dénouement*". Because there is no knot to unravel. Alcoholics drink themselves to death. The depths of Heinz's soul were darkened by *melan cholè*, the black bile relentlessly driving him to his ruin. The wonder was his good cheer throughout.

4

It all started about thirty years ago. I was sitting with my then beloved at an outdoor café on the sea front. Sailing boats festooned with bunting, a procession on the water, the foremost fishing craft bearing a statue of the Holy Virgin, the others crowding round, songs being sung and horns blown, a golden-robed Pope blessing the sea with incense. Heathen rituals dating from long before Christ, because the sea is feared and must be placated, and for that you need priests. We must have been carrying on a conversation, because at one point a flushed, meaty face thrust itself between us, blurting: "I can understand every word you're saying," the kind of remark that leaves you wondering whether you've said anything shameful. No, on that initial encounter Heinz did not appeal. I was put off: he smelt of gin, he was unshaven, and to make matters worse he had just called the waiter to order a drink *in the name of Her Majesty.* So why was that first meeting followed by a second, and after that an endless round of meetings culminating in that final one on his terrace, on a day of slate-grey seas and stormy weather? The answer, I think, is a photograph, yet again. Not the same one, though. It is the picture Molly once showed me of Heinz on their wedding day, his face as yet unscathed by drink, a pirate, a buccaneer, a Clark Gable, a man wreathed in adventure, a freebooter, the type who could get women on every finger because such men emanated a rare sense of freedom, of devil-may-care. I remember staring at that photograph for some time. The epithet "beguiling" is seldom heard nowadays, and never with reference to adult males, but it would suit the tall, well-built figure in the sailing boat holding a glass in one hand and the rudder in the other. The youthful shadow of Heinz Maximilian Schroeder, Her Majesty's vice-consul *in situ*, still in a state of grace, libido and humour intact, not yet overtaken by drink. He was beguiling, and at the same time guileless, to use another of those dying terms. Just a glimmer of mischief in those fearfully blue eyes. A *Mensch*. Apparently I must have recourse to other languages to get anywhere near him. And yet, if I can call him a *Mensch*, why am I so keen to forget what I thought when I first saw him thrusting his flushed, drunken face at me that day? He reminded me of a pig. The bestiary world is filled with hybrids, horses with human heads, birds with women's breasts, Egyptian deities with animal faces, eagles wearing crowns meant for humans, the Minotaur hoisting his weighty, horned head over a human frame that suddenly looks very frail. It was the age of original sin, of the arduous emancipation from the animal state, of the loss of innocence. Our nostalgia for the animal kingdom of old has always moved us to identify, at least in part, with all sorts of beasts, but not to my knowledge ever with pigs, unless you count cartoons with offensive intent.

5

His oldest ploy: an invitation to his beach house, lunch on the terrace by the pool. And a ride in his motor launch afterwards. The launch was a cheap speedboat, the beach house an old fisherman's cottage with stone walls, plastered and white-washed, the terrace three paces wide with a straw awning, the pool an adjoining pond with a knee-high boundary wall; all you could do was sit in it, no question of swimming. It was there that he received his potential clients, few of whom were able to hide their surprise. Any further remark about his pool and he would point to the sea. The cottage was situated overlooking a small bay, and part of the fun was to dive off the cliff, which was not entirely without risk on account of the jutting rocks down below. He was an excellent diver. On my first visit the sea was rough, and his flat-iron, as he called the small speedboat, tugged wildly at the ropes tied to a pair of rusty hooks in the side of a rock. Lunch was what we had come for. Philip had said that my best bet would be to bring a bottle of whisky, so I had one with me. What Philip had failed to mention was that the bottle would be empty by the end of lunch. I don't drink hard liquor during the day, and the women, too, stuck to wine. It was no film, daily life never is, but sometimes it is worth trying to view everyday events in cinematic terms. A curious staginess can then come over the scenes, with conversations sounding as if they were written by a second-rate but not unamusing script writer. The microphone also picks up snatches of dialogue not in the script, the camera pans out towards the rocky island just off shore, then cuts to the head of a solitary swimmer struggling against the waves before zooming in on Molly's white face just as Heinz refers to her as "that shrimp who still can't speak a word of Dutch". Perhaps he was even more pig-like then than the first time, but my transformation was already underway. If it is true there is a kind of love that has nothing to do with Eros and, as Plato maintained, that love does not reside in the beloved but in the person doing the loving, it is also the case that I had already begun to regard this man who was becoming more bacchanalian by the hour, this wild-eyed boozer, with a certain – well, a certain what? Far be it from me to favour the confessional mode, but I shall have to give some account of myself as well. To a circle of intimate friends? I don't really have any. There's just a handful of people scattered over the globe, male/female, who provide the salt of my existence, shall we say. A semi-culinary metaphor, it won't go far, but still. People you mourn when they die, but also, and that's the crux, *prior* to their demise, people you find yourself grieving for even when you are still laughing about them. Vulnerable souls, wounded simpletons, women defying their lot, knights of the sad countenance, men surrounded by a nimbus of disaster. I don't want to know what that says about me, but saintliness doesn't come into it, that's for sure. Perhaps it's compassion, perhaps I'm the dung-beetle drawn to decay, perhaps it's just that the looming tragedy of other people's lives gives me a sense of security, because then at least it's not happening to me. Who's to say?

6

Film. The honorary vice-consul has gone to sit in the paddling pool, and he's singing. A song without words, his life-song, which I will get to hear hundreds of times over the years. A trumpetish tune, like heralds sounding a fanfare for a king. I am hearing it now as I write. The pig's head has become detached from the swine, and emerging from the whisky fumes and layers of fat is the shadow of Clark Gable complete with Bacchus' paunch and moist hair streaked across his forehead. Bacchus, Heinz and Gable are happy. Heinz was possibly the only happy drinker I have ever known. He was a past master at dissimulating his *melan cholè*, making sure he expired before it took over. I give Molly a hand with the dishes, a bit unsteady on my feet. The whisky was expensive, the wine is supermarket plonk, the kind of vile brew that pulls the carpet from under your brains. Molly prepared a tongue of veal, one of those you slide rolled-up into a dish, where it proceeds to lie in state, pinkly embedded in jellied amber, itself heightened by a coded galaxy of lemon-flecks and parsley. He chewed the acidic wine. The shrimp can cook all right, said Bacchus, but that's all she can do – *no, don't worry, she doesn't understand Dutch*. I was not so sure about that, but the English features displayed total reserve. She had practice, and besides – not that I discovered that until later – here was another case of love residing in the one doing the loving. *Elle se maintenait encore en beauté*. Chateaubriand again, this time with reference to Lady Jersey, a name that would have suited Molly rather well. They had two children, both away at boarding school in England, far removed from paternal anarchy and maternal anxieties. In the holidays they returned to the wonderland of limitless freedom, ran around half naked and practised swearing in Dutch, which caused Molly's face, which she kept out of the sun, to tighten like parchment. She found some consolation in having their main home in a fancy tourist ghetto where no-one was ever invited, as well as in the Sunday service at the Anglican church downtown, complete with hymns, a proper English vicar, and an afterglow of nostalgia lasting several hours. For all that, though, she loved Heinz with the same fervour as that which overcame whole companies of English soldiers as they marched into German machine-gun fire at Ypres. She just didn't show it.

Their love-life had been the subject of much talk among the English. There had been displays of high passion, apparently, but that was when Heinz was still Gable, in the days of the undocumented prequel. Lately the gossip tended to be more nastily logistical, along the lines of doesn't his paunch get in the way, you might as well try an elephant, isn't it incredible he still gets a whole flotilla of girls after him when he staggers onto the dance floor blind drunk. False by rote, false by nature. The answer to their mean-spirited speculations, I thought, was simple. Heinz was fun, which is more than you can say about most men. His own explanation took a nautical turn, which was lost on the English. There is no more pressure on my rudder, he once remarked. Plain sailing, no drag on other people either. A bit of dancing now and then, that's fine. I still see those girls, but I pretend they're paintings. Or advertisements. But that was only later.

7

That first afternoon became the template for all subsequent ones. The whisky was finished by the end of lunch, then came the siesta, best described as the mood following defeat in battle: *sauve qui peut*, retreat from Moscow. Everyone literally ran for shelter, because the possibilities were limited. The low wall dividing the terrace from the rocks was not very wide, but that was where Molly lay herself down, in a space between two of the posts supporting the straw roof. She reclined there like a medieval abbess on a ceremonial tomb, the only thing missing was the small dog crouching at her feet with the family crest. Heinz vanished indoors, where the depths of the marriage bed, or adultery bed as the case might be, awaited him. If there were other guests they tended to go down to the beach nearby, but on that first day I was the only one. I had little choice but to stretch out on the concrete ramp leading from the terrace to the outside lavatory.

From that supine position I could see the newly built flats stacked up against the hillside. Heinz had shown me a picture of the place taken thirty years before: Italy still in the shabby garb of fascism and poverty, the days of hesitant reconstruction after the war. No German tourists in those pre-*Wirtschaftswunder* days – they were still busy at home, cleaning up their mess. The hill was a great mass of rock overgrown with scrub oaks, rosemary, euphorbia, thistles and wild garlic, his fisherman's cottage the only building. It was a structure with echoes of Africa, a single whitewashed curve tapering to a point. The adjoining terrace had been his personal contribution to modern times, and now the primeval shape was a solitary reminder of the past among the bleak housing developments in the area. I must have dozed off, because suddenly he was standing over me. He was in his swimming trunks, eyes still bleary from the whisky: how about a dive? Of that too there is a photograph, because his dives were spectacular. He stood poised at the highest point and called me over to take my position beside him. The swirling water down below seemed perilously far away, I saw the sharp rocks jutting out, and was scared. He stood where he was. You'd better start from a bit further down then. That was how it went, for all those years. Him standing a couple of metres above me, me lower down but still terrified of the height, if only because I was not sure how deep the water was. *Deep enough.* I also had to avoid his boat, as well as the mooring ropes. *Piece of cake. I'll count to three.* The photograph shows two divers in mid-air, tuna fish and mackerel, my slight frame contrasting with his massive size. He dived with clenched fists, cleaving the water, and I felt a wave pushing me to the side. He did not surface until long after me, a grinning satyr's head poking out from the shifting planes of grey sea. A happy man, of that there could be no doubt. But that was not the end of my ordeal, next came the promised ride in the speedboat. I can still hear him cheering triumphantly as we slammed into wave after wave, as if we were out to punish the sea. The one being punished was me. I couldn't see for the flying foam, with the flat-iron shooting into the air to land smack on the rock-hard water and me being thrown from side to side, violently shaken, trapped on a death ride going nowhere, at the mercy of a raving, drunken lunatic. I had no wish to repeat the experience after that, not even in the best of weathers and calmest of seas. I had seen him for what he was: a daredevil ready for any reckless deed, as if that might offer a quick-fix escape from the other death ride he had mapped out in his mind.

8

He and I – because I am bound to say a few words about myself, for all that I dislike doing so. You cannot help but discover certain things about yourself in the course of time, things you would rather keep under wraps. You don't succeed, but the wish remains: to take your paltry little secrets with you when you depart this life and close the door behind you. Mission accomplished, whatever it was. Life – can someone please tell me what it's all about? I have long lost track of what "people" means, but I think in any case that the past millennium has been one gigantic striptease for the human species. Ejection from the solar system, Earth banished to the back streets of the Milky Way, brain functions so inflated that we think we know all about the unknowable, God and his helpers dead, and us, the lackeys with erasable names in the service of invisible particles, frittering away our only heritage while admiring ourselves in the mirror. Bombast, you will say, and I agree, so I'd be glad to hear of a more agreeable theory. Either way, I'm at peace with it. For the time being, anyway.

Today the Alps are hiding behind curtains of rain, the trees are already a little greener than when I embarked on this tale without a story. I can hear the rain on the roof and a couple of birds singing for all their worth to make themselves heard, and I feel at one with the universe, if only because it's still there. That seems contradictory to my earlier claim, but it is not. Besides, birds always have that mellowing effect on me. Time was when I thought I was a poet, but I am only a poet when I read. It took me a while to find that out. My first collection of poems drowned in the tidal wave of post-war creativity, and it wasn't until later that I found my true vocation. I became the complement no poet can do without: a reader. There aren't too many of those, not of poetry. Reading can be a profession, but I won't go into that now. I write for my keep. Wood does not make the bed, Aristotle says, meaning that you have to keep things separate. He is right, as usual. A carpenter is not the same as a sculptor, and I am a carpenter. Every quarter I knock together a glossy flagship magazine for some mammoth concern featuring a masthead of a dozen or more fiscal and legal luminaries, none of whom will read the contents. I doubt anyone at all reads them, notwithstanding the lavish expenditure. Offset printing, top photographers and designers, a sprinkling of obsequious legal wizards, and then my own specialism, the Big Names. Not one of them ever refuses, in fact they will queue up for assignments. Give the five leading Dutch writers an abstract theme and five times the fee they ever receive from *de Groene* or *N.R.C.* and their copy comes rolling in thick and fast. The money this makes me goes, unbeknownst to them, towards the purchase of their masterpieces. There are forms of happiness that exclude other people, and anonymity is one of them. Perhaps that was what attracted me to Heinz. He knew something about himself, and it left him cold, or rather, he left himself cold. Which is un-idiomatic, but no less true for that. Sequestered in my tower block on the far side of the Amsterdam harbour, I gather my own Thébaïde, my solitary retreat, about me to do some reading. And since Heinz found me a house in Liguria I travel there twice a year. As I said, a happy man.

9

Feats of arms. A diplomatic incident. The trick with the reading glasses. Fear of the ambassador. The car stuck between two walls. Tollens. Shangri-la. Fishing. The freezer in the super-market. Dutchmen. You name it. Negative heroism, nothing uplifting, never forgotten. The diplomatic incident was ex-emplary, not least because of the way it ended. In his secret heart Heinz was quite proud of his vice-title, especially when he was invited to attend some official event along with other "diplomats". The others, the *corps diplomatique*, consisted of a handful of honorary consuls: a mildewed Englishman, a Spaniard with five names, an American retiree for whom it was a hobby, a Frenchman who ran a shipping company, and a German who, like Heinz, dabbled in real estate. One of their annual get-togethers was on board an Italian navy frigate which sailed out every September to cast a wreath onto the sea in memory of some wartime act of heroism in those very coastal waters. Several sailors had drowned, hence the wreath, and hence the presence of the admiral, the same one year after year, one of those figureheads kept for show. Offering, fatherland, peace, reconciliation, and then the wreath, floating briefly until, weighed down by the wires that held it together, it began slowly to sink, after which drinks were served. It was

September, which meant that the Italians were still wearing those white dress uniforms which set medals and decorations off to such advantage. Someone who was present told me about it afterwards. That Heinz was drunk had not bothered anyone; they all were in the end. Prosecco, Arneis, Barolo, *vinsanto*, *grappa*. It may have been the dazzling whiteness, or something to do with both of them having been divers and sailors in their day, but at one point Heinz had seized a dish heaped with *penne all'arrabbiata* and emptied the contents over the admiral's head with cries of *basta la pasta!* Everybody held their breath. Through their alcoholic haze the others saw how the admiral suddenly turned pale, drew himself up, and declared war on the Netherlands. Then he grabbed Heinz's arm, twisted it behind his back and, holding him close, proceeded to kiss him on both cheeks, causing the thick red sauce to be smeared over them both. Incident closed. Yet more *grappa*. Even without having been there, I could see his face before me. I knew what he was like when he was drunk, the defiance creeping into his expression, the glazed look, the furtive triumph that goes with transgression and risk. The trick with the glasses dated from later times, at the onset of delirium, unsteady gait, tremor of the hands.

He had to make the occasional trip to his native Holland, a country that had grown bewilderingly foreign to him. He would drive non-stop until he reached some small hotel in the region of Macon. A question of hanging on to the steering wheel, he called it. No problem. Plain sailing. Hotel Genteel Poverty. They knew him there, and they knew his foibles. He would be unable to sign the register due to his tremor, his excuse being that he had left his glasses at the bottom of his suitcase so he had to go up to his room first. Upstairs he would make a dash for the minibar, gulp down two miniature bottles of whisky or cognac, didn't matter which, give his hair a quick comb and go down to place his signature at the front desk. Then it was off into town for a proper drink. The other stories were similarly hilarious adventures of structured misery, which increasingly took their toll on his balancing act.

A visit to the embassy in Rome was agony for the same reason, as he would need that drink first in order to keep his hands still. *Don't want them thinking I've got Parkinson's otherwise I can shake it goodbye. And I do need that gilded shield coat of arms and the lions with it. Je maintiendrai.*

10

Why had he ended up living there, on that coast? Chance. Bad boy, drop-out. *All I could do was sailing.* Made it into a career, bringing yachts from Amsterdam and Hamburg to the Mediterranean, the life of Riley, in a way. *Sailing and diving, that's what I was good at. Came over here, stayed. There was a job for a diver on a tanker owned by Onassis, a winter assignment. There's no sailing in winter. Had a look round. Popped into the main café every day. They call it a town, but it's more like a big village. Some old folk in the big café, nothing much. Little old men. I always offered them coffee. Yes please, thanks. They spoke the local dialect. Then one day the bartender said: Signore Cheintz, questi signori sono tutti milionarii. All landowners, this lot. That's how I got started. Later on there were the Germans and the Brits, but the little old men were my friends. To them I'm Cheintz. They would rather deal with me than with those snooty Brits. I know their sons and daughters, and who owns which parcels of land.*

11

But there was another reason. It had something to do with the sons and daughters, but he did not talk about that. It was Philip who raised the subject one day. He made it sound as if he were referring to a distant past, a prehistoric period when records were not kept and dates were consequently vague, a time when the people resembled fantasy figures out of legends or fairytales. Perhaps they never even existed. Heinz had not been alone when he first set foot here. Even that observation sounded slightly off, not like the usual Philip. As if he were tuning an antique instrument after years of disuse. Adjusting the pitch, you could say. There had been someone with him, with Heinz, and her name was Arielle. I could tell from the way he articulated the name that Arielle was not only dead but also that her death had been tragic. I read too much, as I mentioned before. Nothing surprises me. Arielle had been a shining light. While he rambled on it came to me that the light was still shining. She and Heinz, opposites in every respect, an impossible combination. He meant that it was doomed from the start. An unearthly creature, a sprite. He did not actually say that, but I could tell. Someone you could not imagine falling to her death on the rocks, because sprites do not die. She had given art classes to the sons and daughters, and had painted her pupils herself.

Her portraits were still up on people's walls, they had all had them framed.

Everybody came to the funeral, from far and wide, all in black like in the old days. Heinz's stony-faced reaction had caused some consternation. He had gone round to everyone's house to ask if they had any photographs of her, and if so could he have them. Nobody had dared to refuse. It was years later that Philip ventured to ask what he had done with them. Heinz replied by pointing to the sea.

12

So was that it? Was that luminous presence hovering at his side on the terrace in the weeks before he died? Had she been there, too, when he raced over the sea with me, that one, unfortunate time? When Molly gave birth to his children? Was she always there? Also when he started awake from a drunken siesta and stared about him in surprise, as if he had never seen the world before nor had any wish to? Humpty Dumpty sat on a wall, that was a stock phrase of his, and the only way he could avoid a fall was by diving into the sea. Is this too facile? I dare say it is, but then what other means do we have to penetrate the lives of others, to unravel thoughts, crack codes, look behind masks? The paucity we have inherited from shoddy films, and from novels, shoddy or otherwise, the psychobabble spelled out in magazines, the imaginary divans we would never wish to lie on ourselves, all they do is hold up mirrors in which not a single truth is revealed, because the truth is always trounced by the lie. Was Heinz a liar by saying nothing? Did he drink because he never stopped telling lies? Did he have an appointment with death that kept being deferred, and was he relieved when the time came at last?

Here, laughter. Another of his stock phrases, and he was

right. Here has to be laughter, loud and Homeric. I can never resist embellishing. Ever an adjective too many. Here has to be laughter, you idiot.

Stay away from me. But that was not what he said.

13

Arielle. The name came to haunt me back then. I tried to get Heinz to tell me about her once, in a roundabout way, by asking him how long he and Molly had been together, but he saw through me and promptly turned to stone, as Philip used to say. When I asked him about this later, Philip said it wasn't so much a question of turning to stone as becoming hazy. No, he couldn't remember exactly when it had been. She was so utterly gone, he said, the way people you never really get to know are gone when they die. She had been with Heinz when he first arrived, but he had not circulated her – that was Philip's way of putting it. The expression stayed with me because it was so odd – but especially because of the post-humous resentment it conveyed. Heinz had kept her for himself, they had hardly known her, and that, it seemed, was why they had all been so impressed.

She had been striking to look at, and again there was mention of a sort of epiphany, a flicker of light in a pool of darkness, now you saw her now you didn't. And so now she was utterly gone, so much so that it was as if she'd never been there. When I asked what her voice had been like he clammed up. I had overstepped the mark. Voice, voice? How should he know after all this time?

I could see what he was thinking. Why should anyone want to know about the voice of a long-dead woman? It was sick. Grudgingly, he conceded that he had attended the funeral.

It was in the next village, which was where Heinz was living at the time. End of conversation, although it served as small talk at the cricket club afterwards. All those Dutch are crazy. Do you know what that idiot asked me? About her voice, what it was like. And her grave, he wanted to know about that too. Heinz is barmy, but his friends are even barmier.

The grave. My life is never lacking in poetry. I cannot imagine how other people get by. That day I had been reading Montale, who I carry with me whenever I am in Liguria. Cuttlefish bone, cuttlefish skeleton, the book of poems that take place here (do poems take place?). The sun was hellish that day. I had been given directions. Past the church, a long country road with cypresses. "Observe the shapes life takes on when it falls apart," it says in one of the poems, and the preceding one describes what I do. Poetry, however obscure, is always literal. Literal to me, anyway.

I am the reader, I am in charge. "And as you walk in the blistering sun you feel, to your amazement, that the whole of life and its suffering is summed up by walking along a wall topped with broken glass." Over the wall are elm trees, a faint scent of roses, the stillness of the dead. I found myself alone in the churchyard. There was no-one to ask, but I found her straight away. Someone had left fresh flowers. Not Heinz, I was sure. A man who dumps all the photographs of his beloved in the sea does not visit her grave. Small headstone, scant lettering. Arielle van de Lugt, two breaths of air without a sound. 1940–1962.

How far gone can you be if there's still someone laying flowers on your grave after forty years? "Observe the shapes life takes on when it falls apart."

14

There was no point in trying to contact Heinz before ten. After ten he could be found in his office, or in the Bar Liguria, Amleto's tavern. There aren't that many people in Italy called Hamlet, and when asked about his name Amleto would indicate the framed portrait on the wall above the bar. A pulpy face rising from a priestly dog-collar. Between chin and collar a monumental double chin, an uninterrupted slope of flesh.

Amleto, Cardinal Ottaviani. *My father hadn't heard of Hamlet, but he was very clerically minded. He had hopes of me becoming a priest.*

Heinz supplied about half of Amleto's earnings on his own. Whenever I was in the neighbourhood I went over to the Bar Liguria to see him. I had decided not to mention my visit to the graveyard. He was sitting in the back, nursing a large Campari. *My breakfast, my daily bread. Invented by a Dutchman. People round here don't like it if you mention that. Adrianus VI, the only Dutch pope and the last foreign one until that Pole came along, what's his name. Came over from Kampen, brought his own bitters, Campari.*

But Heinz was not in a jolly mood. A Dutchman drowned in the bay, and he could not reach the next of kin. *Swimmers don't carry passports, and all they found on the beach was a basket and a towel. I parked him in the supermarket freezer for the interim. Relatives aren't usually keen to come over, and unless there's an insurance policy they're not keen to lay claim to the body either. So it's up to me. Raises me a little extra cash from the Embassy, but it's not much fun, I can tell you. Come with me tomorrow, and you'll see.*

No, it was not much fun. Hearse with unshaven driver. *Always gives me a steep bill, we go halves.* I acted as the required witness. *I'd have to hire one otherwise and now I've got you.* We followed the dented, black Honda van in Heinz's no less crumpled Fiat. *Last week, on my way home from the disco, I was stopped. Eh! Signore Cheitnz, your house is in the opposite direction! Reversing the car was a bit of a problem. There was a wall there,* which they had put up deliberately for that one night. *They split their sides laughing. But they let me off the breath test. Narrow escape.*

The Dutchman turned out to be a veterinary surgeon, no wife, no kids. A friend who couldn't be traced, a few distant relatives. Oh no, he had always said he was to be left where he dropped, so they just sent a sorry wreath, which, together with the Embassy's flowers and my own contribution didn't look too bad. We walked behind the coffin. It was getting hot, Heinz sweated profusely. August, not April, is the cruellest month in the hills, even if the sea is nearby. Two workmen, cigarettes between their lips, stood by an open grave holding a cloth with a skull, which they promptly set down to shake hands with Heinz. Two gravediggers with their Yorick, eyes glinting with the promise of a tip or free drink afterwards. It was time to raise the lid of the coffin. Heinz drew aside the polythene sheeting. *Look at him!* I looked. Fiftyish, grim-faced, bald. Scowling, as though death had come inopportunely. The moment was brief. Heinz gestured for the men to slide the coffin into the wall. It flashed through my mind that he did not know I had stood beside his wife's grave just a week before.

Rest in peace. Did I really hear him say that? I stared. He was wearing his defiant look. *It's not me saying that, it's the State of the Netherlands. He can R.I.P. here for the next ten years, then the lease runs out. That's it. What they'll do with him after that I have no idea. Ask those two. Grind him up? Incinerate him? Fertilizer? Who knows? I never asked. Weird, eh?* What he meant by this last I do not know. Weird that he did not know what would be done with the desiccated body, or weird that someone's life should end that way, being buried by strangers with no-one at the funeral? I thought of his wife's grave, still extant, so obviously the rent was still being paid. But by whom?

I could hardly ask, not having mentioned seeing the grave. So back we went: Liguria, Amleto *sans* Yorick, lunch down by the harbour, then to his house for some diving, whisky, song, laughter. A cheery vice-consul, no doubt about it. Work done, duty discharged. Fellow countryman planted in a cemetery wall.

15

Dénouement? None. This is real life, clueless and plotless. Drink erodes, assails, wreaks its revenge. Medical dossiers are novels, too. War novels. The human liver can take a great deal, but not everything, not trench warfare, not parachutists behind the lines, not a permanent blitzkrieg. That final summer, just before I left, Heinz had given up smoking. Appointments can be postponed. The rocks surrounding his fisherman's hut were strewn with the plastic tips of all those foul-smelling little cigars I always had to bring him from Holland. *Get rid* of unwanted guests with Wipro. Stopped from one day to the next, just like that. Chucked the whole box onto the barbecue. Cutlet *nicotina. No big deal. Question of willpower. You have to make the decision, that's all.* But the other decision had not been made, or only briefly, half-heartedly. *No more spirits, only the odd glass of rosé.* The odd glass was six bottles. Molly said it just washed through him. *Lemonade. No harm, but no kick either.* The first sign of trouble was in the autumn, when I rang him up. *No, not so good. They've caught up with me.* Who they were he didn't say, but he sounded as if he'd known them for a very long time. *It's all in the game.* I phoned Philip, and could see him shrug at the other end. *He has been working at it all his life, hasn't he?*

He came to Holland. *I have a few matters to see to.* No, he was not a shadow of his former self. On the outside he was the same, but different. Whatever was wrong was happening inside that massive body of his. I had never seen him in a Northern setting before, and his appearance struck me as utterly strange, with his trademark tropical shirt displaced by an old, far-too-tight blazer with brass buttons and a weird badge belonging to a golf club. Old times. But the worst was the face. Teeth twice as long as they used to be, whites of the eyes as jaundiced as his skin. Only the laugh was intact. Unaccustomed to the indoors, too booming for an Amsterdam café. *Just a mineral water for me.* It turned out he had no insurance. Not really. How d'you mean, not really?

Well, none at all. Honorary, don't you know. My friend the internist agreed to see him. Verdict: if he stays over here there's some hope, just a glimmer. But if I'm honest, not a hope in hell.

Hell in the offing. Did you tell him that? Not in so many words, but he got the message. He did not seem surprised. People are either stunned by the news, or they know already. In any case, he refused to stay.

16

He wanted to go home, sit out on his terrace. *Watch the waves for a bit.* He dropped by at my place the day before he left. *King of the castle, eh? You've done well for yourself. What's that?*

That was a mounted photograph of Tonga. What had I gone there for? To write a piece for my mag. About the dateline. His interest was piqued. *There has to be a line of demarcation somewhere, I guess. Never really thought about it.*

So if you take a step backwards, it's yesterday? Depends where you're standing. Step backwards again and it's tomorrow. He wanted to have a try. Drew himself up to his full height in the middle of my living room, stared at an invisible line on the floor and took a step. *Yesterday! Doesn't it drive people crazy out there?* He unhooked the photo from the wall and peered at it closely. Palm trees, whitewashed cottages, a few fishing boats in a small harbour. *That's where I'll go.* He called me up a week later to tell me they had their own king on Tonga. *But of course you knew that already.* From then on our phone calls were all about Tonga. *Must sell a couple of properties first, but then I'm off.* Not a word about his illness. *Oh, I'm all right. Did you know the King of Tonga weighs about a ton? And they have nobles, too. His mother, Queen Salote, was very famous. A giantess, passed her height on to him in width.* And how is Molly? *Molly's with the kids in England.* When are you coming? *October's a fine month over here. Do some diving.*

The real news came from Philip. That Heinz was in bad shape. That Molly had fled. That he just sat there staring out to sea for days on end, and would not hear of any treatment.

People had stopped calling. They were unnerved by the way he waffled on about nothing but Tonga. Strikes me he's losing it a bit, Philip said, come and see for yourself if you're up to it. In the real world I still had a magazine to edit. Deadlines in this context acquired a certain piquancy. Real world is a relative concept, of course, but Heinz's reality knew no bounds. He wanted to start a farm on Tonga. *You can get subsidies for that in Europe. Everything grows there like mad. I can see opportunities for business. Super-healthy food. Cabbage and fish, what more do you want?*

Cabbages on Tonga. I am composed of words, they come to me unbidden. Montaigne said, "I want death to find me planting my cabbages . . . but caring little for it." That death in French is female would have tickled Heinz. And perhaps he was the one who cared little. He never told us. He had Tonga.

17

It was not until November that I was free to travel at last. Stormy weather, my plane had trouble landing. He was not at the consulate, nor in Bar Liguria. Amleto vented his indignation. The son of a bitch won't do anything, anything at all. We've told him we'll pay for the doctor, but no way. We scraped the money together with a bunch of friends, but he pretends not to know what we're on about. He's going to Tonga! So he says! In a coffin, that's how he'll be going to Tonga. Bastard! Shit, crap, *mierda*, followed by the entire faecal repertoire of southern Europe, as if a good mess might yet save his friend. Her Majesty's honorary vice-consul was sitting out on his terrace. The sea was rough, too rough for diving. Heinz greeted me as if he had last seen me five minutes ago. His voice rose up from a death-mask. I could see what his friends found unnerving. His voice sounded the same, but his body had given up. Such a thing strikes fear into the heart. The sea, more leaden than I had ever seen it, pounded against the rocks. It was like that first time in the speedboat, with wild water surging in and out of the small cove below his house, almost whistling and sucking, an invisible giant spitting and slurping, Mother Nature pulling out all the stops of a hundred organs. I watched as the great grey waves rose, gathering momentum for their assault, only to fall back again into a great, receding trough which was instantly re-filled with swaying, leaden masses of water. Because of the din I didn't hear him at first, but Heinz was singing. Singing along with the wind, cheering it on. He looked at me in his old familiar way. He had no need of Montaigne, he was past caring about anything. He was content, or seemed to be. Only then did I see the pigeon, small, grey and bedraggled, huddling in a corner of the terrace. I recalled what Philip had said about him sitting there. *Day in day out with only that stupid pigeon for company. Pigeons don't live by the sea. You never see them. Not crows either. They don't belong there. It ought to have been a seagull, at the very least. An albatross would have been better. After all, they're the ones who signal when the game is over.* Ruffled plumage. The wind, possibly. But in this case it looked as if someone had rubbed the pigeon's feathers the wrong way, they were puffed up, as if it was feeling the cold. Heinz saw me looking. *My lady companion. Drops by every day, ever since I got back from Holland. Funny little bird. Human eyes.* I looked again. The pigeon looked back. But I never know quite what I see in the eyes of animals. Or rather, I see something you can't relate to. You see a marble, or a universe, but that doesn't get you anywhere. Whatever goes on inside has absolutely nothing to do with you. Go to any zoo, stare at a lion, a monkey, an owl for as long as you like, and you won't get a response. For Heinz it was different. *She and I carry on whole conversations.* And then, in the same breath: *I want to show you something.* I could see he had trouble getting out of his chair. He shuffled into the house. A gust of wind swept a large map from the table. Tonga. *Don't fly away. Stop right there.* He retrieved the map and spread it out. We pored over the archipelago. Tongatapu. Toku. Tafali. A sprinkling of 171 islands in the infinite blue of the ocean. He began to hum. *I can't wait.* I stayed for a few days, after that I had to leave. When I went to say goodbye the pigeon was settled on the ridge along the terrace, the very place where Molly used to lie in state. *I told her she might as well stay in England. The* tramontana *always sets her nerves on edge. A lot of brine in the air. Makes everything damp, she doesn't like that. I'm living here fulltime now, as in the old days. The house has been rented out. Gypsy, eh?* I noticed him looking away when I left. From afar I could see him silhouetted against the still bright sky, the shadow of a man with the shadow of a pigeon. Not long after that he was picked up by an ambulance and flown to England.

Andrea gave me the number of the hospital, in a seaside town not far from where Molly's mother lived. I phoned him once. *When I get out of here, I'm going to Tonga. I'll drop you a postcard.* It was only about ten days after his funeral that Molly sent word of Heinz's decease, and of his private burial in the village churchyard. Had him to herself at last. I could imagine the scene. English vicar, English hymns, or how a wayward Dutchman joins the English dead. Philip said the pigeon had returned every day for a long while, and then suddenly stopped. Molly had stayed behind in England. Andrea had cleared out the cottage, it was a shambles, a sort of robbers' den. No, they had not come across a map of Tonga.

18

For several summers that followed I did not go to Liguria. I could not decide whether I wanted to keep my house there. Philip found people to rent it to every season, and Andrea saw to its periodical airing in winter to prevent infestations of mould. Whether Heinz's death had anything to do with it I do not know, but in any case I stayed on the other side of the Alps. I did not return until five years later. After a few days Andrea suddenly asked me to go out riding with her. I am no horseman, as she well knew. *I picked a docile horse specially for you.* Needless to say we talked about Heinz, and about Molly. *Molly's thrown herself into becoming an old lady. She really works at it. A traditional role, been around for centuries: elderly*

Englishwoman in Italy, ha ha. She reined in her horse. We were high on the hill overlooking the village. From there you could see the sea, the inlet with Heinz's cottage. The sea was choppy again that day. She threw me a look over her shoulder, her face tanned and smooth beneath the red velvet cap. She had aged, too, but not with Molly's abandon. She still rode every Sunday, in competition.

Heinz wanted to be alone with his death, it was as simple as that. He didn't need us around. He'd always known that, ever since Arielle. She steered her horse round, the better to confront me. *No-one ever understood what he saw in Arielle. Gossamer.*

I know it sounds crazy, but that's what it was. She was almost not touchable. She was ethereal, if you will, or diaphanous, but will-o-the-wisp is better. A bit like when someone's singing very beautifully, but in the next room. That's why all the men were attracted to her, not least Philip. But it's also why Heinz wanted to keep her to himself.

19

I am back on the other side of the Alps again, where I have been writing this tale. I take a last look at that photograph. The dog, the salesman, Andrea, Philip, Heinz, no-one has stirred. There they stand, frozen in time, but once they get moving they'll be acting out my story.

I peer at Heinz's expression, hoping for some visible evidence of what I have just related. But there is none. The booze, the laughter, the pigeon, death, Tonga – they are all there, but only because I know about them. No-one else does. To them they are invisible. Come upon such a photograph by chance and the anonymous figures will keep their mystery. Their eyes are like the eyes of animals, you cannot get inside them. And what of me? What would the chance observer make of my expression in that picture? The same. Nothing. Or something at odds with reality, whatever that may be. He or she may make inferences about the people's ages, their dress, the fashions and hence the date, even about their characters for all I care, but it is all hypothetical, speculative. Literature, if you will. Invention. We are our secrets, and, if all goes well, we will take them with us to where no-one can touch them.

Late September

Suzy weighs no more than forty-eight kilos these days, so she could do without the fierce wind gusting up the wide road from the sea. Tamarisks, pine trees, ficuses, tossing and rattling. Stay the course, she mutters, bracing her frail left shoulder against the wind. Stay the course, that was what the Vice-Admiral always used to say, the man she had cared for towards the end of his life. That was after the death of his wife, Annabelle, a friend of hers from boarding school. She had made the move from table to bed directly after the funeral. They had slotted Annabelle into the cemetery wall, where now he rested beside her, and then he had driven his old Triumph over to her house in the other village. Back in Wales, where they had originally come from, they would not have acted so precipitately. It was not very seemly, but they had discussed it with Annabelle beforehand, shortly before she tiptoed out of existence. A snuffed candle. Her voice had almost vanished towards the end, but she still managed to whisper in that posh dismissive accent of hers, don't make a fuss about it, we're all so old, the only ones who'll be shocked are the Thursday people and they don't matter. Thursday was the day the Brits held their weekly gatherings in town to gossip, play bridge, and gripe about Spain. Annabelle's clothes, yes, that had been the hardest part. Pringle cashmeres – they were impossible to throw out. She had sent them to the dry-cleaner's and then hung them out in the fresh air to banish the last of Annabelle's Chanel No. 5. He had never noticed. Or maybe he had, but he never mentioned it. And bed these days meant no more than body-warmth, which was fine by her. What the locals made of it all was neither here nor there. He was the *Almirante* after all, a man of standing. Nothing like the EasyJet plebs descending *en masse* on the outdoor cafés to sit around half naked, swilling beer. The language they used was more foreign to her than Spanish. The Vice-Admiral had been no trouble. All he wanted was his *Daily Telegraph* and his Famous Grouse and the opportunity to talk about the war. He had no desire to marry again, and neither had she. She was still in receipt of a pension thanks to her long-dead husband. Also a Navy man, but not of the same stripe. He had put the house in her name so that when the time came she could sell it and move into a little flat in one of the newly built blocks down the coast.

Late September, but it felt more like October. Everything was early this year.

She found it trying, as always. Spain was not a winter country. Come winter and you were thrown back on your Britishness, what with everything taken indoors, terrace doors firmly closed, table lamps switched on for scones and tea with a dash of rum. She paused a moment to catch her breath. From afar she spotted Luis stepping out from the Bar Estrella to see if she was on her way over. The pavement terrace with the metal chairs was deserted, so Luis was bound to be in a bad mood. Yet another day without tips. Four small café tables outside, that was all, but when none of them was occupied the terrace looked quite vast and desolate. Autumn not only meant early evenings, but also that you had to go into town to get the *Mail* – she was not a *Telegraph* reader. She still drove, but had it not been for the newspaper she would have stayed at home. Twice weekly to the supermarket was enough, you could freeze everything. And then there was Thursday, of course, which could not decently be missed. She listened to the sea. The road came to an end in a stretch of grassland by the shore where, in summer, she would find wild garlic, as she called it. Tall stalks with a purple pompon on top. If you poked around a bit in the surrounding soil with a knife you could pull the bulbs up quite easily. He had always laughed at her enthusiasm. The garlic part was tightly packed in a white, papery outer layer, which you peeled off to expose the small hard cloves, each encased in its own brown skin. They were a little sticky, but there was so much satisfaction to be had from things that just grew in the wild. He was not partial to garlic, but she had used a little in her quiches anyway, and it had never seemed to bother him. The ground became stonier towards the sea, until it was nothing but rock, pounded by the waves. When he could still walk he would insist on taking a turn there every evening before supper. They would stand together on the edge, listening and looking. I know exactly what the sea is saying, he would remark, without ever revealing what that might have been. She loved the sound of the sea. Today it was in harmony with the swollen, towering clouds. He was never without his binoculars, in case a ship came past. He would pass them to her from time to time. Today the sea was too rough, not a vessel in sight. She had noticed the fishing fleet lying idle in the bay behind the house, doubly moored on account of the weather forecast.

Luis, whom she had just spied outside the bar, had gone back in. She knew he had only popped out to see if she was coming. That was part of the game, an arrangement they had never discussed. If there were no customers he would stay inside until she sat down at one of the tables. Only then would he show his face. There was no sign of his boss, a hulk of a man with thinning hair in a sorry little pigtail which gave him the appearance of a superannuated American jazz drummer.

In the kitchen no doubt, preparing those tapas she found so unappetizing. Too oily. She glanced inside. Luis was pretending to be busy, setting out small dishes on the bar. That was unnecessary: he knew she would not be ordering anything with her drink, or at the most some almonds. She set her small white handbag on the table in front of her and took out her Dunhill cigarettes. The café tables were a bit cheaplooking, but she liked the way the pearly shine set off her handbag to perfection. The red-and-gold cigarette packet matched her ring, formerly Annabelle's, but hers since he'd given it to her. She took great care of her hands. Pale and veined, of course, but if you used a good nail polish the tracery of blue was less noticeable, and the sight of your hand resting between the bag and the Dunhill packet was actually quite pleasing. She had never been one to care about such things, but now that she had all the time in the world they loomed large in her thoughts. Luis appeared at her elbow. He was wearing a clean brown shirt. The brown shirt was part of his uniform, he never wore anything else. She knew he had no wife, but the shirts were always neatly ironed. Plain black trousers. Black shoes. His feet were dainty. English shoes would have looked better on him than those cheap Spanish things. Just as the Vice-Admiral always knew what the sea was saying, so she knew how the land lay with Luis. Not good today. There was no need for him to come outside because he knew exactly what she would order. That too was part of the game. If no-one else turned up he would stand there and tell her all the things she already knew. Her Spanish was patchy, but she had heard his stories so many times she could have told them to him. Anyway, his English was so poor as to be incomprehensible, so they were quits. She did not need to pay much attention, really, it was like being in church when she was a girl, hearing vaguely familiar words wash over you in the shape of a sermon or litany. Here they belonged to the sea in the distance, to the brown shirt, to his smoothed-back hair, too long at the nape. A year ago it had been the boss's son tending the bar, so the talk had been different then, but he had not returned this year. Not enough custom. She lit a cigarette, thinking she should have brought her pink shawl, the one that had looked so nice on Annabelle. Lady Annabelle. Her hand shook slightly, but that was because of the wind. Luis turned the music down, signalling that he was about to bring her her glass of gin piled with ice and topped with two slices of lemon, and a bottle of tonic water on the side. Two lemon slices, not one – it had taken a while for him to get that into his head. Also that she preferred Nordic Mist to Schweppes. Went better with the gin. They only stocked Nordic Mist as a personal favour to her, as she had been reminded more than once. When the boss was away there would be more gin in her glass, how much more depended on Luis's mood. More if he was feeling sorry for himself, it was that simple. He would start by letting off steam about his first wife, then his second, then his offspring. These last always elicited from him an expression she pondered at length as she lay in bed at night. *Romper la intimidad.* But that would not be until the second gin.

She still hadn't worked out how to say that in English. Break intimacy? Sounded very un-English. But then if she were Spanish she might not have taken to wearing her dead friend's cashmere sweaters. Even today she was wearing something of Annabelle's: a Laura Ashley blouse, pink with a rosebud pattern. God, Annabelle. Plastered after her first gin. She could hear Luis dropping ice cubes into the tall glass and knew she had gauged his mood correctly when he brought her drink outside. There was very little room for tonic water. He had plans. She reflected on her opening gambit.

Not very busy today, is it? He shrugged. One sentence from her warranted at least ten from him in response. Doing ten to the gallon, was how she thought of it. No indeed, the season was crap (*temporada de mierda*). He wished he had never set foot in this place. It was still hot and sunny in Seville, but out here it was already winter. Only yesterday the boss calculated that takings were 6,000 euros down on last year. He cursed the day he had seen the advert. But now he had applied for another job, over in Oviedo. If his first wife hadn't bled him dry he would still be running his own bar. Oviedo – they drank cider there. Horrible stuff. But then they weren't real Spaniards anyway. There were still bears roaming the mountains in Asturias. As bad as Siberia. No place for a Sevillano.

But it had not been up to him. Fate had dealt him a rotten hand.

She took a first gulp. This was the high point of her day, when the world was transformed. She could feel the blissful contentment coursing through her veins. A fitting counterpoint to his *lamento*. No sooner had she picked up a cigarette than he snapped his lighter. Too much wind. Fucking island, he grunted, to get the ball rolling. I reckon we'll be shutting down early this year. She could hear the statement lurking underneath, which would belong to the second, no less gratifying gulp: then you'll have nowhere to go, you old English cow. She thought a moment, drew on her cigarette, blew out the smoke from the side of her mouth, and in the same breath uttered the response he was waiting for: oh no, surely not? But he was already firmly on track. The children. Living in Mallorca, they were, but he was not welcome there. She took a sip in anticipation of what he would say about his offspring, and also of the face he would pull as he said it. A question of *romper la intimidad*. His children had *intimidad* among themselves, which would be disturbed by his presence. He, who had cared for his mother under his own roof until her death at eighty-four! But there was none of that shit about *intimidad* in the old days. Least of all with his first wife. In any case, she scarpered when his mother died. Didn't fancy keeping house. He went inside for a clean ashtray, but she knew it was really for a quick slug of whisky behind the bar. She counted how many cigarettes she had left. Hm. She did not like the brand he smoked. Singed cardboard with white filters, felt dry on the lips. The perfect cigarette for the likes of you, you clown, she thought, and said, well, I hope you'll stay open for a while yet, it will be so quiet without you. She peered into the packet once more. Only three left, and she wasn't going into town until morning. Just then an open blue convertible came speeding down the road. It halted with a screech of tyres at the edge of the sea. Pity they didn't drive straight on, growled Luis. We could do with a bit of action round here. The car did a U-turn, came back and pulled over at the terrace. German number plate. Deafening music with thumping basses and a woman's high-pitched wail, like a torture victim in a machine factory. Any chance of a meal? That meant the whole thing would be delayed. She added some more tonic to her gin. She'd have to try and stay awake. Watch a film on Sky, maybe.

Or should she have another drink? The Germans parked their car, and at once the sea was audible again. Funny to hear Germans without Spanish trying to communicate in English. Sounded like a war film: *Jawohl*, sir.

Luis brought them two beers, hovering ingratiatingly. That was for her benefit. He didn't need her, that was the message. When he finally shifted his attention to her he began by going over the same ground as before the interruption. Did she know Oviedo at all? No, she did not, nor did she wish to know anything about it. If you go there I shall come and visit you, she said, and began slowly to rise to her feet, teetering in a sudden gust of wind. She had already put down the money, with a saucer on top to keep the notes from blowing away. Luis turned his back on her in favour of the Germans.

Stay the course, Suzy, she muttered. At least no-one would think it was the drink making her unsteady. But no-one was looking. She put her hand to the wall for support. He seemed to be ignoring her deliberately, which was odd, but she resolved to leave him a little something anyway. That was her forte, placing small offerings in his path, tactfully and with discretion. A silver teaspoon on the table, the decanter of Famous Grouse by the telephone, things like that. Plain cash was too blatant. There had to be some refinement to the gesture, as well as an appearance of fortuitousness. The last time things had got a little out of hand. He had helped himself to Annabelle's silver cigarette lighter. That had not been her intention, but she had said nothing.

Arriving home she found she had left the television on; she could hear it burbling away as she came into the hall. She paused on the threshold of her sitting room. The light in here is too harsh, she thought, better switch off that floor-lamp. Should she get ready for bed now or should she wait?

Nothing would happen before midnight in any case. She watched television until three people were gunned down in one fell swoop, then made her way to the bedroom.

As she climbed into bed it occurred to her that she had not left anything for him to find, but by then she could already hear his footsteps on the garden path. She did not leave the outside light on at night, no need for him to be seen. Hallway, sitting room, a cat prowling in the dark. A sixty-three-year-old Spanish tom-cat in black Spanish shoes, which should have been English shoes.

All that remained was to wait for the creak of the door, the smell of whisky on his breath, those strange, halting grunts accompanied by sudden thrusts of astonishing vigour, which had more to do with rage and endemic disappointment than with anything else.

It was broad daylight when she awoke. She listened to the news on the World Service. Baghdad, Darfur, Gaza, Kabul, in one ear and out the other, but she found comfort in the newsreader's civilized tones painlessly easing you back into daytime. She had just turned seventy-nine, and had listened to the news as long as she could remember. There was always the news, just as there was always the weather to ruminate on. She dragged herself out of bed and went over to the window.

The sound of the world came from the radio, but the sight of it was right there, before her eyes. A deserted road strewn with dead leaves. The wind had dropped, with doggish obedience. All was as it should be.

Her white handbag stood on the coffee table, wide open. Her purse was empty. She tried in vain to recall how much had been in it.

You little shit, she thought, and on her way to the kitchen to make herself a cup of tea she sent a nod to the silver-framed photograph of Annabelle on the large desk. In the ashtray beside it lay a stubbed-out cigarette with a white filter. Annabelle smiled back from the realm of the dead, an ambivalent, half-indulgent smile. But then, with Annabelle, you never knew.

Last Afternoon

And then suddenly he was dead.

She would always remember the moment, because of the imagery that came with it. September, slanting sunshine, the shadow of the cypress reaching the wall at the bottom of the garden, the tortoise waggling slowly towards the hibiscus bush in search of the first bloom to drop. This was an agreement between her and the tortoise. Always the last hour of the afternoon, which was simultaneously the portal of the evening. The reason why darkness falls earlier here than in Holland is that Sardinia is closer to the Equator, he had explained. Light had been a sensitive issue with him. Light was alive, he referred to it as if it were an unreliable associate who frequently did him a bad turn. Some days were hateful to him on account of the light, not that she could see anything wrong with it, of course. That was a feeling she had had from the start, that he was affected by invisible things, things she could neither reach nor put a name to. They had been together for three years. Their previous worlds had never overlapped, all they had shared was the desire to live abroad, and the ability to work from home, here in this old farmhouse. He had appeared in her life by sheer happenstance: a man on horseback who glanced over the wall into her garden and waved when he saw her.

She had been attracted by the way the things he said were somehow at odds with what he did for a living (finance), as though there were a poet lurking in the depths of his large, solid frame. He had been good in bed in a rather gauche sort of way, she mused, the same as he had always been good with his horse.

She watched the tortoise. There were several, but this was the only one she always recognized at once. That had been another disparity between them. One day he sat down to explain to her how to tell them apart. He scooped up a tortoise and set it on the table. The creature quickly retracted its old man's head so that only the shell remained, which he proceeded to stroke with both hands. There, he said, and there. She had peered at the markings and tried to see the patterns he pointed out to her, but coming across a tortoise in the garden next morning she had been unable to tell whether it was the same one. This particular tortoise she knew because she had put her mind to it. She had taken a colour photograph of it sitting perfectly still under the hibiscus bush. Afterwards she enlarged the image so that the shell would fill the entire frame, a print of which hung in her study. An abstract painting, friends had commented appreciatively, why don't you make some more of them? She knew that was what he had thought as well, although he had never said so.

The tortoise was now within nosing distance of the hibiscus. It seemed to have a preference for the flame-red bush, leaving the yellow one a bit further on to its fellows. She had been surprised by their fondness for flowers, as though there were an insurmountable barrier dividing the ethereal, delicate petals from the fossil-like antiquity of a tortoise. The hibiscus was her favourite flower. It was also the only plant that needed care in summer aside from the luxuriant plumbago and the bougainvillea, both of which required little or no watering, and likewise the only one to make a daily gesture of acknowledgement, as it occurred to her.

In these latter years the summers had become dryer – with occasional hosepipe bans – but in her garden that caused little inconvenience. Aloes, cacti, a yucca branching out in every direction, palms, pines, and that single cypress – they were all self-sufficient, extracting the little moisture they needed from deep in the ground. Only the hibiscus produced fresh flowers daily, blood-red blooms resembling butterflies unfolding their wings with wondrous alacrity when she got up in the morning, only to die at the end of the day and fall to the dry brown earth, as now.

Everything about tortoises was strange. The way hers was now lumbering towards the fallen flower on its archaic front legs and turned-out feet reminded her of a crab. The flower had furled itself up like a winding-sheet before it dropped, as though in readiness for what lay in store. The watching woman felt a frisson. She ought to have grown accustomed to this daily ritual by now, but it still gave her a vague sense of pain to see the tortoise touching its armoured head to the flower, which was no longer red, but rusty, the colour of dried blood. She saw the inscrutable beady eyes, she saw the strange lipless maw opening and the jaws begin to grind the flower, and again, just as she had fifteen minutes ago when the shadow of the cypress reached the stone wall, she felt certain: the man she had lived with for years, and who had died a few summers back, was now truly dead. He had taken his time, she thought to herself, but she knew what he would have said. He would have turned it around, she could hear his voice, his light, somewhat condescending irony gaining an extra edge after the first gin and tonic: "It's you who've been taking your time, my dear. Was it so hard to part from me?"

Same hour, same set-up: woman plus tortoise, tortoise plus hibiscus, man plus gin and tonic. "To arm myself against the evening."

She had found it perplexing, a man who feared the evening because he feared the night. But it was true, parting from him had not been easy. She sipped her drink.

"Look at you, taking on my bad habits!"

What could she say? That they had already been miles apart when he was alive, but that it did not mean he was dead to her when he died? It was only now, at this mysterious moment of the cypress's shadow creeping up against the garden wall, that he was dead to her. How could you be so sure about something like that? There had in fact been three such moments, she reflected: the moment he left, that of his dying, and the present, long-drawn-out moment of beginning to forget him, of his passing into a shadow of himself, his real death.

A shadow of himself. She savoured the phrase. A shadow free to roam, over the wall, past the fig tree, over the next wall and then across the neighbours' field, where just then the donkey began to bray as though greeting him.

That sound had been another sensitive issue: the heaving, sustained braying which spoke of immeasurable sorrow, and which always ended in a strange sort of grumbling noise by way of a coda to all the grief.

How simple everything was! She kept perfectly still. Whether the tortoise was looking at her she could not tell, but its head was cocked towards her as it continued to munch, a last remnant of russet trailing obscenely from its mouth. A moment from now it would pause, shift each of its four stumpy legs in turn and slowly trundle away out of her sight. Its home would be somewhere along the stone wall, but she had never been invited to visit. Yet another creature that had no need of her. She laughed, and heard her own laughter in the stillness of the garden. No answer. Just the faint rustle of palm fronds. Tortoises start life below ground, she told herself, which is where the dead belong. Perhaps this one visited her because she had unearthed it herself, but you could never be sure. It had happened when she was hoeing, suddenly there were two, three tiny tortoises emerging from the turned soil. She had been amazed, but he had explained about the tortoises' subterranean infancy. Then he had picked them up and tossed them over the wall. Cause and effect. Was it possible to pinpoint the beginning of an end? And if so, did that moment come when you first wondered what you were doing with a man who tossed tortoises over a wall, who was intimidated by light and afraid of the evening? She wrote books for children, which she illustrated herself. That day she had started a story about three small tortoises, to which she had given his three Christian names, but she had never shown it to him.

Her revenge would have been lost on him anyway. She had to think of something more drastic, and in that she succeeded beyond expectation. Catching his wife in the embrace of Beppo the postman was bound to do the trick. The pretty-boy postman who came by each day on his racing bike, the man he offered glasses of wine, the man he discussed the sins of Berlusconi with, the man who watched the Pope's funeral on television with him, who passed on the village gossip, who hung out at the Bar Italia – yes, that one! Right there in the meadow among the thistles, under the fig tree, and you riding past on your horse, hearing a noise, glancing over the wall, seeing the brown, suntanned back with the head of black hair and the blonde hair fanned out below, the wide blue eyes, so very Dutch-looking, staring up at you without a trace of fear or shame, meting out punishment for three dead tortoises and three years of irony.

It had grown dark, but still she sat without moving. That she was laughing nobody could see now. On that day she returned a few hours later to find him in his office scanning his computers, as ever linked up with global stock markets. She stood behind him, watching the abstract ciphers ripple across the screens. That was the moment of separation. The next day he went down to the gate as usual to collect the post, had his customary glass of wine with Beppo, and then left the house without a word. Not long after that he died, as though by mutual agreement, and now, this afternoon, he had finally vanished over the garden wall, as if he had never existed.

She stood up and went into the house. Passing through her

study, she touched her hand to the tortoise picture. She heard her own footsteps on the way to the kitchen and stood still a moment, listening to how quiet everything was.

Paula

1

Ghosts I do not believe in, but photographs are another matter. A woman wants you to think of her, and contrives to make you come across a photograph of her. The dead, if neglected for too long, can affect you that way. Or perhaps I should say: if they *feel* neglected they can affect you in that way. In my case neglect does not apply, because I still think of Paula pretty often. I don't know about the others, I hardly ever see them these days unless by chance. Gilles is dead, Alexander got his degree in the end and is now a medical inspector for the social services in Groningen, Ollie has moved to the States, and the Doctor's an invalid, last I heard. So that is not much use to her, because she is without doubt one of the unquiet dead. It's down to me, then. Perhaps by default, but nevertheless.

Alright then, Paula, here I am, remembering you. I'm good at that, always was.

Because I never stopped. It's an eternity since I've been living on my own. Excess baggage disposed of long ago, but there seems to be no real end to it. I keep finding more. Top-floor flat in a modern building, sparsely furnished, quiet neighbours, peaceful, views over the wide polder landscape. People seldom visit, when they do they look about them warily like cats scanning the surrounds for danger. Bed, table, chair, all streamlined. Minimalist, remarked the Baron with that pale smile of his, that one time he dropped by. He had come on account of an old gambling debt, stood there with the air of a bailiff assessing my possessions in case I didn't cough up. I had no intention of coughing up, not then, and not now. I had been expecting that visit for years, I knew he'd turn up eventually. Old habits die hard. I'm not sure how your memory fares these days, but I have no doubt you remember the Baron. Seeing you two dancing together was always a treat, especially to the Rolling Stones. Old men themselves these days. He'd go into a sort of mechanical trance like a wound-up robot, with you rippling and swirling around him, but he always linked up at the supreme moment, and the result was a pulsating machine that drew everyone's eyes. As my eyes are now drawn to you. Your photograph, propped up against my white wall. Well I never, there's Paula, said the Baron when he was there. Long time no see.

Reminds me of a Zen monastery, was another comment he

made, but I have never been in a Zen monastery. I just wanted to keep things simple, no clutter, just bare, white space. I'm getting there. I don't entertain, so one chair for reading is enough. Same one for reading and eating. All my walls are white, as you may have noticed. No idea what your sort do or don't see. I detest looking at photographs of me when I was young, but it may not be the same for you. You are incapable of ageing, so you've never looked any different. How many years has it been? Forty? Forty-five? You made the cover of *Vogue* magazine, and we were all bursting with pride, even the girls. Nothing about the picture has aged, not you, nor the photograph itself. Last year you suddenly turned up among some newspaper cuttings from the old days – Provos in Amsterdam, love-ins, sit-ins, all that stuff. It's hard to imagine any of it actually taking place. I was busy for months, it was like a military campaign. Suitcases, cupboards, folders. That steamer trunk with the diaries was the last to go, and that's where I found you. All earmarked for the incinerator, with the exception of the photograph. You standing behind a closed window, left elbow raised against the frame in such a way that the just-lit cigarette between your fingers is slighter higher than your head. You wouldn't see a model smoking on the cover of *Vogue* today, nor would the fingernails be so short. It was a brazen, sexy image then, and that still holds today. Thin, boyish body. A white bandeau wrapped around the torso, no doubt a fashion statement at the time. Intimations of a double mastectomy. The boobless wonder, said the Baron. The Writer used a more flowery expression, borrowed from some poet whose name I don't recall. Dark hipster trousers, right hand in pocket, skin sprinkled with the raindrops clinging like tears to the windowpanes, your face looming out from the dimness beyond, lips slightly parted, gaze directed out of the picture. I can't look at it for very long. There you are in the realm of the dead, and yet you are about to speak. I can hear you now, that voice we will all remember to the end of our days, the hint of rawness, hoarseness, drink, cigarettes, a kind of aspirated prelude to your utterances. Har har, and then you'd be off, working your wiles not one of us could withstand.

A lethal weapon in poker games, that voice of yours, capable of turning a lame hand into a full house.

2

I have taken my chair and am sitting in front of you. In a home with only one chair that means something. I have put your photograph up on the windowsill with a couple of smooth beach pebbles along the bottom edge to keep it in place. It's wet outside, which fits in with the raindrops on your windowpane. This way you have rain in front of you as well as behind. I have this idea you can see me, but I suspect it is not the case. Which is probably just as well, because you might not even recognize me. That is also why I'm not saying these things out loud, although it's in contradiction to our face-to-face arrangement. I never hear other people's voices here, and no-one hears mine. I think.

It was the Year of Our Habit. That is what we called each year back then, because we were hooked, and we knew it. A shoe-less evening was a waste of time. I can still feel the touch of the cards when I held the bank, I can feel it, and I can hear the sound. When you first arrived I was also holding the bank, left hand resting on the wooden side of the shoe, right hand poised, fingertips on the first card. The game is more generally known as baccarat or *chemin de fer*, but we had our own variant with our own rules, and we called it shoe, that was enough. It was shoe every evening, including that one. The room was dimly lit except for the table, which stood in a pool of light so the only faces you could see properly were those of the players. The doorbell rang, someone went to answer it and those of us who were not playing looked up expectantly. There was a hush, something which only happened when strangers turned up, people we did not know. You arrived alone, which was unusual, but no questions were asked. That was not our style. Much as we disliked interruptions, we broke off to shake hands, that's when we first heard the voice. Cinco had given the address, you said. Cinco, remember him? The perennial loner? Checked tweed cap, used to prop up the bar at Hoppe's? One-time city councillor for Traffic Safety because we had all voted for him. Har har. Cinco, who stopped coming after a while. Dead. This will be my refrain, I'm afraid. Can't be helped, it's part of my life nowadays. I lifted my hand from the shoe and set the stake. One hundred guilders. Perhaps I was just trying to impress you, it was still a lot of money back then. André was sitting to my left. Normally cautious, this time he called *suivi*. I drew the cards, inspected them. Two nines and a six, excellent hand. Over the players' heads I looked at your face, eager, covetous. And I was not the only one: the Baron, Giles, Nigel, even Tico and the Prodigy were looking, too. This was duly noted by the womenfolk, standing by with hackles raised and claws at the ready. It took a while for you to get them under your thumb. No, that's not right – to get them to love you the way we did. Har har. To the women your laugh sounded different: hoarser, deeper, sweeter. I held the bank ten times or so. Two hundred, four hundred, eight hundred, *banco* each time, till I could "take chocolate". You were a fast learner. *Banco suivi, banco avec.* Get it in the neck. That was ever the Writer's response, we expected it. You lost time after time but in the end, when the stake was back to eight hundred, you called *banco*.

The hubbub subsided. I drew the cards slowly. You held them as you must have seen them do in films, tightly together at first, as if they were one card. You raised them close to your chest, still as one. Only then did you slowly lift them to eye level, spreading them fractionally, just enough to check the values. Har, you said, meaning "a card". That was the first time I lost to you. From then on you were one of us.

But that is putting it mildly. It was more like you had always been one of us. Paula? Oh, known her for years.

Years? How long that period lasted I do not know, but what I do know is that everything shrivelled after you died. We followed somewhat from a distance what was going on in the rest of the world: Vietnam, riots in Amsterdam, squatters, cold war, the H-bomb, the Club of Rome with its apocalyptic forecasts, the first oil crisis, Prague '68.

For most people the real war was still quite recent, clearly there were new conflicts which would bring even greater calamities, but, as Nigel would say with cool assurance, those calamities would be on a very different scale from what all the current fuss was about. We believed him, which probably had more than anything else to do with the fact that he always won. Besides, we had other things on our minds. Nigel's field was mathematics, where order reigned. The world was chaos.

We were rather vague, the whole lot of us, but the game was crystal clear.

Dodo and Gilles lived in a canal-side house in the southern part of Amsterdam. The canal was a poor imitation of the old ones in the centre, and more of a boundary between the city and the new suburbs that were springing up back then. As the Writer used to say, it was like having to cross a moat to gain access to their castle. Writer was his real name, and that he wrote for a living was a bonus. The Baron had introduced Wintrop, his associate in vague dealings with stocks and shares which they never discussed, not even with André and Gilles, who played the stock market themselves, or had done, that never became clear. Nothing was clear, really. There was no hierarchy. The Jewish Prodigy was studying to become a surgeon, Nieges dealt in dodgy antiques, and Merel ran a small travel agency with third-world destinations from a little office in the Pijp neighbourhood. Nigel, whose name jarred with his appearance of someone languishing in Dostoyevsky's basement, was studying maths, paying his way by playing poker at a private club from which we were barred. Tico was an agent for Chartreuse wines and an obscure brand of Champagne. The Doctor owed his name to having dropped out of medical school. Remember them? Ollie was with André; she stayed in Texas when he died. Absent friends and the dead, such are my companions.

Merel and Tico are still together, apparently. Like me they lead what I call shadow-lives, or rather, like me, they never came out of the shade. There were those of us who earned real money, those who already had it, and others like me who scraped it together here and here, but money was never an issue. How you got by I never discovered. You did some modelling, but not on a regular basis, and yet you never seemed to be out of pocket. The Writer published books we didn't read, the Baron was a district judge somewhere, the Jewish Prodigy became a successful surgeon though he didn't like to admit it, Merel's agency flourished when immigration from Surinam took off, but money was never discussed, not by any of us. Nigel kept the records of the debts, which amounted to endless rounds of figures being cancelled out against each other. We were all permanently in debt. Every few weeks Nigel would say it was time to settle accounts, which would duly take place the following session.

3

So what is it about remembering the dead? Yes, I know, I won't get an answer to that, nor to the question I really want to ask, which is, How is it that the older you get the more your life begins to look like an invention? Hard to say which is worse, getting old or being dead, but then you have never been old and I have never been dead.

I think the reason I have made the place so bare and empty is that I don't want my invention to bear any resemblance to anyone else's, though that's nonsense of course, because at best it'll only be another invention, one that you do not come across that often. You knew all of those things all the time. You were an avid reader, but there was always a niggle, as if there was always something missing. It was from you I got that idea about invention. We had been to see a film, which I found moving, as I remember. Almost the real thing, you scoffed as we left the cinema. Everything is a copy of something else, it's hardly worth living when some guy can come along and squeeze your whole life into a ninety-minute feature film or a book you read in two days. To each his own novel, I say, but even that would take too long. Imitation, that's all there is. I believe I was shocked, in any case I was lost for words. You went on to say something about time being compacted, and I could almost feel it happening. We were walking from Leidseplein to Vondelpark, where the gravel underfoot intensified the sensation. Our steps keeping pace with physical fact struck an accusatory note, as if they were clamouring to be conflated into a film sequence or into a line in a novel like every other. Nigel, who rarely said anything remotely personal, once remarked in the middle of a game, Paula, you're in too much of a hurry to live. Nigel, another conquest. Nigel, who was having an affair with Dodo, who was married to Gilles. A whole pile of novels. You tried us all, tried all the films. Maybe Nigel was the only one you ever really cared about, but maybe not. So mysterious-looking with that white face of his, was all you said on the subject. He was the only one you couldn't have. You had me, easily. There was no mystery about me then, there still isn't. I went all out for you from that very first evening, and that was a story you'd read a hundred times already. The only time we made love you answered my transparency with yours: I don't see what's so special about fucking. *C'est un geste rendu,* no more than that. No less either. And afterwards you said: evidently you and I were not made for each other. Don't look so miserable, this is only the beginning. Good to get that out of the way. Best friend I ever had. It wasn't you saying that, it was me, and yet I never really knew how you felt about me. Sometimes you gave me a look as if you were hiding something. Three weeks out in the Niger desert, by jeep to Tamanrasset. You came up with the tickets after you'd fleeced us all that unforgettable night when it all went so fast Nigel could hardly keep the score. You were holding a bank that seemed impossible to break, the chocolate steadily melting over the table in your direction. Shoe, *banco, suivi,* chocolate. For the unthinkable contingency that you might have forgotten, chocolate was the profit you could take out of the bank if the stakes were too low. *Banco* meant you only wanted to place a bet equal to the bank total. *Suivi* meant you bet *banco* again after losing. The trip was unforgettable. I still spend some time in the desert, any desert, every year. En route you made out with one or two stray men. I won't embarrass you, you said, I'll say you're my brother. In which case I'll have to slit their throats, I said, you don't give your sister up to the first caravan that comes along. But we had agreed: no jealousy. That was the deal.

I spent such evenings writing my own story, alone in a tent, dogs howling all across the oasis. My only pride was that it didn't resemble any stories I knew. Whether you felt the same I don't know. You made no comment, just gave an angry, rapacious look, as if you were left wanting.

Were you unhappy? What a crap question, you'd have said. Then, quickly, an arm round my shoulder, and a whispered – you could whisper, too – I wouldn't have gone on a trip like this with anyone else. Wouldn't and couldn't. If you fancy a fuck just say so, we have all the décor we need right here: heart of Africa, palm trees, camels, stars. Har har.

4

The Baron owed his nickname to his renounced nobility. His grandfather, a believer in egalitarianism, had wrought his own little French revolution by dumping his title in the dustbin of history. It was a loss that caused his grandson to suffer phantom pain. He still had a family coat of arms, but no title to go with it, so he cherished his surname all the more for its noble ring. You know all that. The dead don't have Alzheimer's.

You needn't listen, I'll carry on talking anyway. For my own benefit. To furnish my space. I don't miss them, for all that they were dear to me. Tico called me Don Anselmo for some reason, I think it had something to do with a film we'd seen together, "*El Cochecito*". Tico and Merel. He had a touch of the Indies about him; the formal, overseas accent still lingered. Father in the Colonial army. Sergeant, but no matter, formality assured. Colonial hang-ups. Forever insecure about making the grade. We're from Madura, if you know where that is. Think Bali, Lombok, Soemba, the whole Indonesian archipelago. And Timor, half-Portuguese. People forget that. Tico was friends with Nieges. Ah, Nieges, expert on the patina of age, remember? A question of chemicals. Bury an item in the ground with a drop of this or that and it'll age all on its own in no time. Tico didn't obtain his degree, but knew enough to be of assistance to Nieges. They saw each other during the day, which I found odd. Alexander was busy with his internships at the same hospital where the Prodigy worked. Merel, Dodo and Ollie were involved in something they'd call fitness now. The Doctor spent his days in chess cafés. I never saw any of them during the daytime, for me they belonged to the evening. The circle of friends, the faces in the yellow lamplight, the smoke. And you. I can see you before me now, nothing to it, one can project any image one likes on the polder. Which reminds me of what you said about time being compacted, because things went too slowly for you. Perhaps it was just a throwaway remark, which I'm blowing out of proportion. And yet. I have the time to think about such things now. The first film I saw by Antonioni was with you. Antonioni and Bergman, both of them dead now too. It's as if I never saw another film since. I lost interest. In those days it was all left-wing radicalism, you were supposed to show solidarity with any number of causes, sign manifestos, march for peace, outrage was mandatory. That didn't bother us much, but the indignation was everywhere. University buildings occupied by students, rebellion in the theatre, sugarcane cutting in Cuba, marches for Cambodia, police crackdowns, and all that time we were busy with shoe and *banco*, a bunch of deserters washed up on an island. No trace of all the general mayhem in those films, which is probably why they made such an impression on me. They were not about social issues, just about people. Individuals. A distasteful word to me even today, but no matter. Solitary souls. Someone riding a tram going down a deserted street. The solitude amid the turmoil. 1964, 1965, I'm not sure. *Il deserto rosso*. Monica Vitti standing with a man at the base of a towering metal scaffold, two tiny figures, so small you would think they were nameless. It was then you dug your fingernails into the palm of my hand. That's exactly it, you said, we don't mean a thing. Who do we think we are? We're being shredded, erased. Our stories are the same everywhere, they have no meaning. I now have that film on D.V.D., and several others. I watch them at night in here, where I'm sitting now. And each time that scene begins I can feel your hand. Antonioni spins out the moment, the wasteland, the wall, the metal framework, the agonizing diminution. That evening you didn't join us at the gaming table. I was holding the bank with considerable success, and at one point I looked up. You were standing behind the Prodigy, your expression curiously intense, you gave me a little nod and at once made a gesture with both hands drawing in the entire circle, two quick waves and a swipe to the side, as if you were throwing us all out of the window.

After that you left.

5

Our famous escapade took place a bit later. It was the Baron's idea. There was an uncle somewhere near Rouen where he was to deliver something or whose signature he needed, I forget which. So then why not make the most of it and have a go in a real casino, at Deauville? Not everyone was available. The Prodigy had weekend duty, Ollie wouldn't let André go. That left ten of us to pile into two cars: my old Renault 16, the Baron's cat-back Volvo. Move over, Don Anselmo. You were in the Volvo, next to Nigel. It was strange seeing them all in broad daylight. The Doctor had a mildewy look. Belgium was grey. We made a detour to Saint-Omer, because Nigel wanted to see the church labyrinth there. I have never felt much at ease in churches, least of all Roman Catholic ones. Nigel and you were already there. You were standing at the centre of the labyrinth, which extended across the nave like some strange board game. I still have a postcard of it. From his hand gestures I could tell he was tracing the paths in his mind.

His face was very white; I don't believe he ever saw the light of day.

I was too far away to hear what he was saying, but he was talking a lot, contrary to his taciturn habit. I say, Paula, got some breadcrumbs? called Tico, visibly startled by his voice echoing through the church. I watched you trying to follow the path out of the labyrinth and not succeeding. It's getting dark, folks. That was the Baron. He had been against the detour, but had been voted down, everybody insisted that a labyrinth in a church was not to be missed. Why is this region called Picardy, Dodo wanted to know, there's nothing picaresque about it. Not a knave in sight. Just the lingering smell of war.

Two wars, Gilles said. Graves in their millions around here. And it's not Picardy.

The light was slowly fading. The trees lining the road had white bands painted around the trunks, which lit up one by one. The rain drummed against the windows, inside the car all was quiet. It wasn't until we arrived at the casino that we all woke up. *Il Barone*: ties on. Yessir.

Entrance hall, fitted carpets, chandeliers. Passports, entry forms. I glanced round at my companions. A scruffy-looking bunch. I don't know about nowadays, but back then entering a casino was quite intimidating. There was a gravity about the place, a solemn atmosphere of destiny and fate, addiction and castigation. And of sheer, unmerited luck. I said so out loud, and you, standing in front of me in the queue, looked over your shoulder and said: some people are born better-looking than others. Our names were entered in imposing ledgers. I always think they'll refuse me entry, Tico said. We queued again for chips. After that we all dispersed, as though by prior agreement. Superstition, not wanting to stand close to anyone you knew, not wanting to push your luck. Nigel made for the poker table, which I didn't dare. Casino poker was out of my league. Gilles and the Baron opted for baccarat, which came closest to our shoe, while the rest of us sought out the roulette tables. You stayed by my side at first, watched the bets being placed and said: yet another labyrinth. After that we lost sight of each other. It was a large space, and it struck me that we had spread out like an army patrol combing enemy territory. Roulette was a game I think I always played to lose, which was, paradoxically, the only way I occasionally won. Not that night, though. I did what I always did, a pathetic combination of adventure and caution. French francs, a hundred of which seemed a lot of money back then. Oh for the days of the quaint old currencies! Guilders, marks, lire . . . I staked a hundred straight up on twenty-three, and another hundred on red. I knew I'd carry on like this until I ran out of steam. Twenty-three could be trusted not to come up at all, and if black came up a couple more times (*no earthly reason why it shouldn't, statistically speaking, Nigel would say*) I'd stake all my remaining chips on a random number. In retrospect I realize I was aiming to lose, just to get it all over with. Because what I really wanted to do was watch. Very few people gamble for fun, there's always more to it. You can tell by the twitching muscles in jaws, the sidelong glances, the way a player suddenly stands up to leave or gives an over-generous tip. But the croupiers held a special fascination for me, the dealers of fate and doom, the spine-tingling undertone of metaphysical ennui in their voices. Big words, Don Anselmo. Sheer boredom, more like. *Mesdames, Messieurs, rien ne va plus*. Still one of the best sentences ever spoken. The flurry of last-minute bets, split on two-three, split on zero, then the final, prohibitive, *rien!* The baleful stillness until the white, spinning ball drops and bounces, a sound without comparison. Two kinds of players, those who look and those who listen. *Cinq, rouge, impair* and *manqué*. What was that you once said at Dodo's? You were holding the bank, your hand on the cards, no more bets, ladies and gentlemen, here goes: cancer, car crash, divorce, misery, love and passion, a diamond as big as the Hilton . . . Nobody laughed. We weren't stupid, we had already thought of that ourselves.

After half an hour all my money was gone. I saw you in the distance, side by side with your fate, but we were not to know that then. He raised his Champagne to you, you clinked glasses. You struck up friendships wherever you went. I did not go over to you, but wandered off towards the other tables. Nigel, white as a sheet, as ever. Dostoyevsky in Baden Baden.

Even he lost. Gilles and the Baron had already left the baccarat table. Tico turned his trouser pockets inside out and held them wide between finger and thumb. The Doctor had a piece of paper covered with scribbled figures, his unbeatable system, but lost all he had. Only Dodo and Merel were still playing. If we all end up losing, said Tico, we won't have any money for petrol. Go and tell that to Merel, we said, tell her to stop, she's still got chips. But Merel refused: she wanted to take her own sweet time going broke.

In the end you were the only winner. The rest of us, losers all, had gravitated to your table. No credit cards in those days, no money out of the wall. Stop now, said the Baron. That was the wrong thing to say. You gave him one of those special looks of yours, took a sip of Champagne. We stared at your stack of chips, trying to guess the value. Ten thousand at least. For Chrissake, Paula, save some for our dinner. We didn't much fancy your new friend. He had tattoos on the backs of his hands. Miniatures, a bit like the runic signs they brand into bulls. He said something to you, and you laughed. As if you'd known him for ever. An accent, Spanish or Italian. You motioned to the croupier, circled your finger round the pile in front of you and then pointed to twenty-three, which had just come up. My number. He raked in the chips, totted them up in a flash the way croupiers do (like stirring a pile of shit, the Writer said later) and exchanged them for larger, higher value ones. He held one up to check your approval. It was a gold chip. Everyone was watching now. You nodded. He slid the chip towards you, and prepared to send the remaining, lesser chips after it with that obscene, off-hand croupier's gesture saying it's not money lying there. But it is money. I could hear Tico groaning under his breath when you signalled keep the change. Damn, there goes our dinner, he hissed between clenched teeth. *Pour les employés, merci Madame.* What about us, then? Aren't we in her employ? I have always wondered what sort of relationship croupiers have with money. They don't get their salary paid in chips, after all. Very few of them play. They've seen a thing or two. All eyes were on you. *Faîtes vos jeux.* Tattoo placed a stack of chips on the table. A top-line bet on the zero with one, two and three, to be precise, then he filled the corners, and finally put a high-value chip straight up on zero. You didn't move, just stood there holding your golden chip, and I knew what you had in mind. So did Tico, apparently, because I could hear his stifled moan: No, Paula, no. But you had already done the deed, with slow, almost priestly deliberation. Twenty-three. My number. Zero came up. No-one spoke, Tattoo was the only player with stakes on and around zero. So his payout naturally included that golden chip of yours. A thousand francs. Had the twenty-three come up you'd have made thirty-five thousand. The croupier pushed the mound of winnings over the table towards Tattoo, who fished out a gold chip and slid it towards you. You accepted it without batting an eyelid, as if you and he had been at it for years. You did not exchange looks. *Faîtes vos jeux.* Tico let out another moan, a dog mourning its master. Nigel was watching, so was Merel.

The atmosphere was tense. Then came the old flicker of complicity between the croupier and the player, a female player, because it only happens with women, really. A game of eyes. Just a fraction of a second, an attempt at exorcism which everyone knows is futile. The force of the hand sending the numbered wheel spinning round, the ball bouncing, skittering, bouncing again until it finally drops, caught in the small cell with the sacred number.

Twenty-three. Things moved at high speed after that. It still hurts to think that those were the last moments we saw you. You slid your winnings to the man beside you, who slid them back: thirty-five thousand, just sitting there. Tico moaned again, Nigel stared at a point over our heads, Gilles lit a cigarette. You nodded to the croupier, pushed a chip in his direction, divided the thirty-four remaining ones into two equal stacks. Meanwhile Tattoo stood up, waited. You turned round, kissed Tico, kissed Merel, kissed me, ran a fingernail down my neck, handed one of your stacks to Dodo and dropped the other in your handbag. For a rainy day, you said to no-one in particular, and stalked off with your man. Much good it'll do her, murmured the Baron as you vanished through the revolving door. We all knew you wouldn't be back. You had left your stake on the baize, pointing to me. I ought to have pocketed it, instead I placed the gold chip on red. Black came up. There are no secrets.

Outside, it was still raining. Someone suggested taking a walk along the beach.

The girls weren't keen, so they stayed behind in a bar-tabac on the boulevard near the casino.

Gusts of wind, and the other sound, that of surf. For a while we stood there getting wet. Then Tico said: I didn't like the look of that guy. Nigel made no comment, neither did I.

Ever woken up in a French seaside resort in the off-season? Hotel Sleepless Nights, hangover, view of the sea, gulls, driving rain. *Petit déjeuner* with apricot jam and those little wrapped squares of butter from Holland. Six months later: Hotel Corona de Aragon in Zaragoza goes up in flames. Pictures of people behind the top-floor windows waving their arms as if there's a party going on. Eighty-nine dead. Nearly all Spanish, a few Germans, a Colombian, and one Dutch national. Just one.

Paula II

You called me, and here I am. Whether you can hear me I don't know. The chemistry between us is not something I can control. Perhaps it passes through your skin, by way of that photograph which you propped up against the window. You weren't talking aloud, and yet I recognized your voice. That is the kind of chemistry I mean. I am learning a lot here. To begin with, nothing whatever that I had imagined about death turns out to be right. That is the first lesson we learn. I say "we" – that is an old habit, because I am on my own here. There must be an infinite number of dead around, but they are absent in their own deaths, as I am in mine. I am no longer a body, not any more. It never occurred to me that there might be nothing for me to hold on to. No substance. No light, no shadow. No temperature, no time. Did I say here? There is no here. I do not believe I can explain. There is nothing in front of me and nothing behind me. I am still alive, but there are no circumstances. It took me a long time to work that out. How can you say long, if there is no time? I wasn't provided with a new language, so I'll have to make do as best I can. I cannot see myself, but I know I'm here. Without a body. There is nothing surrounding me. Not even space. When I say I heard your voice, it is the truth. If I say I am still present, that's true too. Perhaps I should not try to explain, just try to describe what it is like in terms meant for you, terms you can understand, even if you do not understand the situation. I am completely alone, like all the other dead whom I can neither see nor hear. I am my memories, to be sure, but how long I can hang on to them remains to be seen. Only when they are all gone will I be truly dead, that is what I meant when I said: I am still alive. I have died, but there is life in me yet. It feels as if I still have to finish something. Perhaps it is true that we hover around for a bit in places familiar to us, perhaps that is why we still have something to say. Or fancy we have, and that someone can hear us. I still catch myself thinking in terms of my physical body sometimes, but mainly as a lack. No, a loss. To say phantom pain when your whole body is no longer there, that is pushing it, I know, yet it must be something like this. But there is no one way of getting it right. I remember being deeply moved as a girl by the legend of Odysseus in the Underworld, beset by pale spectres, meeting his mother. Well, it's not like that at all. No-one's coming to visit, that much I know. We have to work at a past even as it slowly slides away from us. No future for me, only past. Past that no longer belongs to time, past of a different category. You have to understand that from now on all my words are approximations, adulterations, endeavours to continue speaking in your kind of language. Maybe it could even be that we are dangerous company. There are peoples where the name of a dead person is taboo. He has no name. Her name is never to be mentioned again. In Japan the dead are given a new name. I too, for all I know, may have a name like that. I no longer have a place, a where, a when.

But let me begin with the moment of my death, which was not like anything you people thought. There was no supernatural aura, let me tell you. It was a hotel fire, with all the panic that that entails. A mass of flames, terror, then smoke. I didn't suffer, in case you want to know: I lost consciousness. I just drifted out of life unawares, you could say. Quite a transition, but hardly dramatic. I remember being very astonished. One second later I was here. Later, one second, a tick – forgive me my anachronisms, but I cannot talk to you in any other way. There is one thing you ought to know. I have heard everything you have been saying and thinking in this room. Don't ask me how, but thoughts can make themselves heard, too. You never understood the relationship we had together. You believed the lie I told you. Women are good at lying, men at believing. Har! Going on with you would have meant giving myself over to your essential absence. That was always painful.

That is also why you are still on your own after all this time, I recognized the signs straightaway. You aren't essentially there for other people, staying together would have been a complete disaster, which I would have survived, but not you. You had to live in order not to be there, or you had to be there while not being there. There are such people. When I say essentially, I mean that literally. I have always loved words. Essential and being are very close.

Our Saharan journey was one of the high points of my life, I can say that now without exaggeration. That one time we slept together I had to leave you with the delusion that for me it was only a quick fling. What was it I said? Something about a *geste rendu*. Forget it, or rather, don't forget it, just one of those strategies people use to deal with the impossible. The glow deep down was so searing, so savage, that my death was nothing by comparison. You did not notice anything, men are very good at that. Now, you think I'm exaggerating, but I have no reason whatsoever left to exaggerate anything at all, not where I am. Where – I still cannot unlearn the language. The un-place I am in. That better? If I am not mistaken, I am finishing my life. Strange that it is only possible in this way. And then I also have the feeling that I have to get a move on. I do not see colours, but if I could they would be slowly fading away.

I admired you no end. There, I've said it. I loved the lot of you, Dodo most of all maybe, but I loved you all, really. A wayward bunch, not desperados, but still. My footloose friends, who still managed to make their way in the world, though their heart wasn't in it. I used to watch you all closely. Take your Zen monastery – I saw it coming miles off. Forgive me for saying this, for someone still among the living you make a rather dead impression, as though you have taken an advance on your mortality. All this bareness, the stark white walls. I have no eyes, but I can see anyway, I hope you can stand the paradox. I can also see my photograph. It is not painful, but it does excite a huge nostalgia. Har har, I can hear you thinking of my voice. I knew I could bewitch you that way. You and Dodo. I had an affair with Dodo, but none of you ever knew. With her, I could have a rest from all those men. Yes, from you, too, even if it was different with you. You I had to let go. I said none of you knew, but it is possible the Writer had his suspicions. He was seeing a lot of us, you included. I was always afraid he would write about you. Hung around for years waiting for his book and in the meantime he watched, collecting. If you are a watcher yourself, you know about these things. When I was with Wintrop I could see how he was following everything closely, only just avoiding writing it all down when we were there, in those little notebooks he carried around with him. One day I sneaked a look at one of them: *P. Voracious. I. W. and Don Anselmo her born victims.* Dutch words in Greek script, a puerile grammar school code which happened to have no secrets for me. It is all there in one of his novels, as a matter of fact: *thief for friend, thief for lover,* something like that, a whole list. He was always hovering, set on bedding me if the opportunity arose. Wintrop did not mind, he was greatly amused by the Writer's imitative skills. He did not even resent him when the book came out, thankfully without me in it. He said you were a mystic. *Watch out, he's the king of denial, the authentic black hole. Mind you don't fall into it.*

I said I had to let you go, but was that really the case? You will find this hard to believe, but I think I was just frightened. Am I sorry now? Did I peer into an abyss and lose courage? Was I too cowardly, too weak? When I was still alive I had resolved never to have any regrets. Now I don't know anymore, but that is probably because it is too late anyway. Too late, another of those irrelevances. I know even as I speak that it is nonsense. Too late, regret, even you no longer deal in those notions, for all that you are still among the living. What I am after is remembrance, but what I get is inventory. That cannot be right. There is still too much of me, I need paring down. Wiping out.

Air, I need air. It is strange, but I am losing concentration. I promise I'll be back, but just now I feel as if I am fading away. I am as good as dead, but there is still so much I want to say.

Is that possible, being dead and yet feeling so tired you think you're dying? Dissolving, fading, vanishing. Ghost – another favourite word. Is that what I am now, a ghost? Some words are unmentionable here: physical love, ecstasy, that kind. A glass that can splinter at a glance. The memories I no longer have, the ones I can still summon. That song of Richard Strauss – the last, I believe, of the *Vier letzte Lieder* – ending with: *ist dies etwa der Tod?* That question, that's what it's all about. Borderland, no-man's-land. But Strauss was still alive when he asked the question: *is here death?* Vague, and yet incredibly accurate. Rest in peace. The dead cannot rest, and lonely as I am already, my loneliness must yet increase. Can you still hear me? Can you still see me, my photograph, the polder landscape? What was that you said just now? Rain inside, rain outside? Rain! I remember exactly when that picture was taken. There was a night with Nigel – yes, he too, even if you thought not. Nigel Algebra, cool as they come. Still, a night. Cries and whispers, sweat, love, pain, and then flight to Dodo, balm, healing. And drink, and coke, and the following morning that photographer, the window, the rain, the picture you are still looking at. With love? To me it is bewildering. *Vogue.* That was me, wasn't it? *Was* – what an insane conjugation! I'll be back, I said, but are you sure you want to hear more of my poor secrets? All those men, all struggling to work their way inside, as if they want to be born again in reverse. They are on top of you, and all such a body can express is a desparate form of will towards cunt, cunt, all it is is forward thrust and always expelled, that's what it is, isn't it? They're all so different, and so the same. Horrible, and no, not horrible. Life seems such a big deal, it is only afterwards that you find out how transparent it is. A spider's web. But also how sacred it is, oh God no, I mean, if anyone had said anything like that to me in the old days I should have cut him short. Har har. Isn't that what it's all about, cutting out the sacred? *The sacred*, do you hear? Alright then, why not have a go at being dead yourself? How much time (forgive me) do I have for this farewell?

Sleep. You have slept. Me, I have lost the ability to sleep, but what else to call it I don't know.

My speech has been reduced to feeble comparisons. I am talking about the feeling you get in some hotels, with the lights dimming very slowly. It was a bit like that. I simply waited, without any sense of anticipation, for the lights to come on again, just as slowly as they had gone down. I saw you sleeping. You can't blame me, you're the one who started all this, it was you who called me. You were restless, fearful, in your sleep. So much for your Zen monastery, it is no use deluding yourself. I can remember how restless your sleep was out in the desert. I can remember exactly what you told me. You always woke up at about 5.00. One night you went outside and stayed away for a long time. I followed you out. It was very cold, I could see your breath in the air. There were myriads of stars, more than you ever see here, a whole sea of infinitely distant other worlds, signs, shapes, scrolls in the incredible stillness. After a time I plucked up the courage to ask if anything was wrong and you told me not a night went by without a moment at which you no longer wished to be alive. You tried to sound ironical, but you did not succeed. You were afraid of that moment, because you knew it kept coming back. I could hear the fear in your voice, you don't fool me. Not then and not now. Afraid of the dark. And then you said something I have never forgotten. *The Foxes come at night.* Something your grandmother had said a lifetime ago, when you were still a child, and you never forgot it. Nor did I. We stood there for a long while, I wanted to end the silence but could think of nothing to say. Foxes. When you had gone back to sleep I saw them. I could hear them sniffing and scrabbling around the tent, panting softly, their nails on the canvas, I could see their jaws half open, their sharp little teeth, their sly pointed faces silhouetted against the tent. I could hear them talk. Do you believe me? I cannot tell you how many there were. I never saw them again after that one time. But I knew you were never without them. Once you have heard someone say they do not wish to live any more, you cannot help wondering who the person behind that statement is: the man who makes everyone laugh, the man who can imitate all kinds of animals to perfection, the man who can shuffle cards like magic, or the man of the foxes who once upon a day does not want to go on living.

I deeply see you. You did not know much about me, none of you did. I used to sing in a choir, even you were not aware of that. Yes, contralto of course. Darker voices weaving in and out of the high-strung sopranos. The high notes are the most passionate. Warp and weft. Surely you, a lover of language, can see what I mean. I too have always loved language, Dutch being my personal favourite. I had spent some time at university, studying Dutch, which none of you knew either. No-one cares about the vanishing of words. Worst of all is the language expiring along with the speaker.

Weft, do you know what that means? It is what you call the threads that cross from side to side when you're weaving. That is what my voice felt like – the dark weft when the sopranos need tempering. It is never the other way round. Exaltation has to be kept in check. That was my role. It is the low tones that keep the ecstasy from flying out the window and getting lost in space.

Composition as a means of banishing hysteria. Order. God, how you'd all have laughed to hear me say these things. But I am free to say them now, that is the advantage of the lucidity. My senses are all alert – another of death's gifts. Forgive me if I sound high-flown, but I have no other voice. None of you had eyes for where I was coming from, you were all too firmly ensconced in your own private domain. Am I being too harsh?

Why did you all get together every night? What your transcendence came down to was laughing so as not to cry, if I may say so. I saw it all. I know it sounds arrogant, but it is true. There were those I came to know in bed, frogs and peacocks, civil servants and crackpots. What you all had in common was your defiance. You defied Fate, if not in the real world, then at least at the gaming table. Losing was one of the realities we lived by, while each win, however small, stayed our acceptance of that truth.

But I also saw the cheating that went on. The nine tucked into the cuff. The sleight of hand. Do you want me to go on? But you knew all along. The Jewish Prodigy, light-fingered. A gold coin, a silver propelling pencil, returned the following day by his girlfriend, remember? That time we had dinner with that friend of Wintrop's, a Dutch diplomat or some such. No, I'm not upset about losing, it's just that gold pencil belonging to my father, I can't understand where it's got to. The next day he had it back. The girlfriend again. The Prodigy had been in hiding during the war with strict Protestant farmers, shifted umpteen times from one family to the next, impossible lad, but he survived. Learnt to lie and steal. Took his revenge later on, which we covered up with the mantle of love. The invariable taunt when he held the bank and the stakes were high while he was all set to take chocolate: *you can afford that, can you, or am I going to have to wait forever and a day?* Ah, you lot kept me well busy. Funny how nobody ever asked what I did in the daytime. My days were spent recuperating. Doctor, nurse, whore, priestess, psychiatrist. And posing for the occasional picture, for the moolah. I had my choir practice, too. And for the rest it was all you, you, you. The amazing thing was that you all kept mum. Anyone angling for gossip was banished to my personal Hades and henceforth avoided like the plague. You wouldn't know about that, because you never asked any questions. Gilles, who did not know I slept with Dodo. André, soon to be dead, who would have dumped Ollie in the canal for the privilege of dying at my side. Nigel, ever adding and subtracting, now reeling with Alzheimer's. Tico, *amuseur général du peuple,* the only one just as funny in bed as out. How many men would think of tricking out their erection as a Muslim bride? Some gauze bandage and a dab of lipstick and Fatima was off, dancing across the hills and dales of the sheets. Doesn't all that seem indescribably flat now it is all in the past? Should I have chosen a worthier path in life? NO. Something a bit more in the vein of the Bach cantatas I used to sing at the Lutheran church on the Spui, which none of you ever came to listen to? NO. Should I have ventured into your abyss to see how you tried to destroy me? NO. I stole a march on you. Once a day you would wish you were dead, but all your livelong day it is me who's dead. You could not have lived with me anyway. Am I wrong? Were you my life's challenge?

It's not getting any easier. Do I have all day? There is no day. I have today. Insane. You would think a dead person had more power. That you wouldn't have to make do with stale bread, broken instruments, obsolete concepts. My lights are going down again. I am only rambling on like this to stay close to you. I have to finish this, but cannot find the ending. I have been watching you the whole non-existent day, alright? Your extremely slow life. How you gazed out over the polder. I know you've read *Purgatorio*, but I could not see what you were thinking. After that you sat very still for a whole hour. You got up to straighten my photograph, and I felt a rush of nostalgia for my body, yet again. You all had it at some time, so it never really seemed to belong to me. I do not need it back, the memory is probably worse for you than for me. I watched you, and your existence struck me as harder to bear than my lack of it. Come over here, I wanted to say, but I do not know where here is, and even if I did, there won't be anyone else there. Not a soul. You'll see.

One last thing I want to tell you. I sank away. I did not burn. That last brief moment, for want of a better word, I could still see. Arturo, that was his name. Arturo was suffocating, and in his distress he grabbed the T.V. aerial. You used to see them in hotels, a bit like nickel-plated antlers. The T.V. was knocked off the table in the process, dragging him down with it to the floor. Your mind can actually register the craziness of such a scene, did you know that? A big, strong guy sprawled on the floor beside you, hugging a T.V. That was the last thing I saw. Then the other kind of seeing began. I slept, or something like it.

A sense of great peace. Take me at my word, it might help later on. But my hair.

I had never given my hair much thought. It must have been the most ephemeral part of me, I suppose. I saw it more vividly than ever before, and I was suddenly overtaken by such a love of myself, as if I had never got round to paying heed to the person I once was. I had missed myself, all those years, I only found myself at the very last. What I remember of it is a feeling of insane love. Can you imagine? Suddenly I realized who had died. It was me lying there on the floor, with the stupid light from the flickering T.V. screen on my hair. It was cut short, as in the photograph, but it was shiny, silken. I wanted to stroke it.

One last time, the very last. It feels like being blown away by the wind, and having to come back each time from further afield. You are the only one who has really called me. The others thought of me from time to time, but none of them could find me. Their grief, if that is what it was, lacked energy, the distance was too great. Just one more thing. Arturo, now, he was so far out of your league. But not out of mine, you see. He touched a chord with me. When I walked out of that casino I had already become someone else in your eyes. Everything was wrong about him except his force. You all despised him. I saw it in your faces as we left. Dodo in shock, Gilles and the Baron staring in disbelief. The Writer lusting after a story, a story. The novel of a chameleon. Well, the story unfolded alright, but it will never be written by him. When I for you was instantly transformed, I remained the same. Perhaps you were the only one who understood.

My fingernails pressing in your hand that time, watching Antonioni. Then a fingernail in your neck. Leave-taking. The last goodbye. You have opened your window. Gust of wind. That was me. Rustle, whisper. The sound of foxes, a night in the desert. Imaginary foxes. Not real ones. All very fleeting. As we are. Gone.

The Furthermost Point

That is not for women, my father used to say, it is always men aiming for the furthest point, never women. But I would not listen. There are more such points to be found on an island than on the mainland. My favourite furthermost point here is Punta Nati, particularly in bad weather. Seeing the trees in front of my house bow down low to the *tramontana* tells me it is time I went over. I get my rain gear on and head out of town. It is not a large town, so before long I find myself in the outlying industrial zone. I see workmen busy moving crates and boxes with forklift trucks, which, when reversing, make a high, monotonous sound, as if they are in pain but not allowed to show it. I can still hear their plaintive drone as I set off on the narrow road going north. The wind has increased to gale force, making me keep my head down like a servant. It rips through my hair, looking up into it even for an instant leaves me blinded by tears. The road is lined on either side with walls made of the stones that lie strewn all over the plain. The rest of the island is green, only this corner is barren. No trees. The occasional bushes are sere and tough, their scraggy forms uniformly listing to the south in obeisance to the wind. The sheep roaming the area find little to graze on. I know it is a two-hour walk, but I never pay attention to time. A minute or an hour, it is all the same to me. What is it you're after, my father would ask. He is dead now. I wanted to explain, but never could. It is only when I'm there that I know the answer, but afterwards it is gone again. An expanse of stone. Thunder, clouds marbled streaks of pale sky, beneath which the plain lights up with a strange glow. Dead gold. Over the ages the peasants cleared their fields of the scattered stones, which they piled up in mounds that serve no purpose. I imagine them being lived in by people unlike any of us, but I know it is not true. There is not a soul here, there never is, and the lands that were once farmed have fallen into disuse. The road comes to an end at a lighthouse. The tower is unmanned, the pavilions at the base unoccupied, the great revolving light switched on automatically at sundown. The site of many shipwrecks in the past. I know the names of those ships by heart, and I recite them as I walk, like a litany. The lighthouse grounds are not open to the public, but I know a gap in the boundary wall that I can slip through. Drawing near to the cliff edge I hear the sound of the sea, both rage and jubilation. I have come to dance, which is not something I could ever have admitted to my father. My partner is the wind, holding me, pushing me this way and that, brusquely irresistible. I give myself over to its lead, risk being knocked to the ground. The rocks around here are jagged and sharp, they cut and bruise me sometimes, injuries I always had to conceal when I was a girl. There used to be a path leading from the lighthouse to the inlet where you can see the waves churning down below. Just a faint track nowadays, since no-one comes here anymore: the ground is uneven and treacherous. There is nothing to hold on to for support, but I want to go to the very edge anyway, I want to be part of the ecstatic fury. Mayhem is what it is, war, peril. Shifting planes of grey being heaved against the rocks. Swells of water forming great arcs, hollowing themselves out within as though striving to fly up into the air. The grey offers a whole spectrum of shades, from bluish and glittery like petrol to the pitch black of a funeral pall. Paroxysms of rage, sprays of foam erect in mid-air, stark against the grey sky, then lapsing into the trough of blackness gathering itself for a renewed, redoubled assault. Whips cracking, giants roaring. That is what I have come for: the roaring. I muster my courage – I know there is no-one to see or hear me – and begin to roar back, waveringly at first so I cannot hear my own voice, but then louder and louder, rage against rage. I scream like a hundred seagulls, I shout to the sailors who drowned there, call out to them, they answer me, I know that is my yearning, to be lost in all that swaying motion, and I know it is not possible, that the dance is over, that I will trudge all the way back again, pursued by the lashing gale, mortified by my own debility. I have lost the north wind, we say around here, *he perdido la tramontana*. Which amounts to saying you have lost your wits, of course, but in my case that does not apply, because I have all my wits about me. I was happy, but there is no-one I can share it with. I have to wait for the storm and the sea to summon me again to the furthermost point. That is our understanding.